Cherry Cream and Murder

Holly Holmes Cozy Culinary Mystery – book 4

K.E. O'Connor

K.E. O'Connor Books

CHERRY CREAM AND MURDER

ISBN: 978-1-9163573-3-4

Written by K.E. O'Connor

Edited by Amy Hart

Cover design by Stunning Book Covers

Beta read by my wonderful early review team. You're all amazing.

Chapter 1

"This makes a fun change from the bike, doesn't it, Meatball?" I glanced over from the driver's seat of the white van I drove.

"Woof, woof!" He wagged his stubby tail in complete agreement.

I grinned to see my fabulous corgi cross perched on my friend Louise Atkins' knee as we headed into Audley St. Mary to make a large delivery of cakes for a posh party.

"He's having a great time," Louise said. "And I can't wait to see this house. I've never been inside Marchwood Manor."

"Same here." I pulled the van to the side of the road to let a bus squeeze past. The roads around the village were mainly single lane, and I was used to racing about on my delivery bike, not driving one of the vans. But we had thirty trays of delicious treats to deliver to Sir Marchwood's party. They'd never have fit in the trolley I used to deliver cakes around the village.

Meatball bounced on Louise's knee and leaned forward, his pink tongue poking out. He was secured with a safety harness to the seatbelt Louise wore, so was perfectly safe.

"Holly, look!" Louise wrapped an arm around Meatball as she leaned forward in her seat. "They have unicorns at this party."

I slowed the van and squinted. Sure enough, there were two enormous creamy gray horses with elegantly styled horns strapped to their heads. I felt a bit sorry for them. I doubted the horses wanted to dress up for this event. They were magnificent enough without the fake horns and glitter on their skin.

I stopped the van by the entrance gate of the manor house. A large security guard walked over with a clipboard.

"Holly Holmes and Louise Atkins," I said. "We're delivering cakes for the party from Audley Castle."

He checked his clipboard before waving us through. The double gates opened in front of us, and I drove along the private road toward Marchwood Manor.

The manor house was almost as old as Audley Castle. It used to be owned by the Trevelan family, but was now looked after by Sir Richard Marchwood. He hadn't been here long, but was already known for his extravagant parties and VIP guest events. And it looked like he was adding unicorn themed parties to his social activities.

As happy as I was to be here and have a look around such a beautiful place, I really wanted to get back to the castle. We were hosting a huge event of our own, and one that was right up my street. It was a three-day history program and was just coming to an end. There had been fascinating talks, exhibits, and demonstrations of medieval weaponry.

I loved learning about the past. There was something so fascinating about how people used to live and how it shaped the way we did things today.

I parked in our allocated spot and climbed out of the van with Louise.

"You'd better stay here," I said to Meatball as he tried to sneak out the door. "You don't want to scare the unicorns. And Sir Richard may not like dogs."

"Woof." His little nose lowered.

I unwound the window and pulled a doggy treat from my pocket, which I handed to him. "You won't miss out on anything. And we won't be long. When we get back to the castle, I'll take you for a long walk this evening."

"Woof, woof." That earned me a small wag of his tail as he munched on his treat.

I walked around the back of the van, opened up, and started unloading the cakes onto the two trolleys we'd brought with us.

"Are those my party cakes?" Sir Richard strode out of the castle. He wore a green silk cravat under a pristine white shirt and black suit pants. He had a broad smile and a twinkle in his blue eyes.

"That's right, Sir Richard," I said. "Where would you like them?"

"In my hand. I always enjoy Audley Castle treats." He smiled at both of us. "Are you just delivering, or did you make these?"

"Holly makes the best treats in the castle," Louise said. "She's our baking genius."

"That's excellent news," Sir Richard said. "I insist on the best for my guests. I invited the Duke and Duchess to attend the party, but they told me they're hosting a history event."

I pushed the loaded trolley toward the manor house. "That's right. It's been a great event. We've had speakers from all over the country, including Professor Stephen Maguire. He's an expert in Tudor knights and medieval warfare."

"I've never heard of the chap. I always enjoyed English at school. That's what I studied at university." Sir Richard flipped open the lid of the top box and peered inside at the neat row of cherry cream tarts. "Mind if I try one?"

"They're all yours if you want them," I said.

"Don't tempt me. I have a terrible sweet tooth." He pulled out a glistening tart and took a bite. His eyes closed, and he groaned. "Absolutely delicious. My guests will be so pleased with these. Right this way. I'm at a loose end at the moment, so I'll show you through to the kitchens."

We made short work of unpacking the rest of the cakes, and after two trips to the van, the back was empty, only the faint smell of sweet pastry left behind.

"Before you go, here's something for your hard work." Sir Richard came out with two full glasses of what looked like champagne on a tray and two cherry cream tarts.

"That's very kind of you," I said, "but I'd better not have the bubbly. I'm driving."

"I'll have yours." Louise grabbed both glasses and took a sip. "This is delicious."

"And of course, you must have the tarts. Unless you get to overindulge in the kitchen and you're sick of your own baking." He passed us the tempting treats.

"There's always room for something sweet." I took both tarts, since Louise was busy downing the champagne like it was water. "I hope you enjoy your party."

"Thank you, my dear. I always do," Sir Richard said.

Louise made short work of the champagne before placing the empty glasses back on the tray. "Thanks. That was amazing. Even better than they serve at the castle."

"I won't tell the Duke that. He always claims he has the best wine cellar in the county." Sir Richard chortled before waving us goodbye as we climbed back in the van and drove away.

Louise hiccupped as she held the tarts and balanced Meatball on her knee. "How the other half live, eh? Think how much it must cost to heat a place like that."

"Probably almost as much as it does to heat Audley Castle," I said. "These old buildings are beautiful, but they take a lot of maintenance. I'm happy in my little apartment."

I had a small apartment in the grounds of the castle that came with the job. It had one bed, a tiny kitchen, bathroom, and lounge, but it was all I needed. Just Meatball and me, happy in our little piece of paradise.

"Shall we take a break?" Louise said. "We got unloaded quicker than I thought we would. Chef Heston won't expect us back for a while."

"Ten minutes won't hurt," I said. "And Meatball could do with a comfort break by the looks of things."

He was bouncing up and down on Louise's knee again, not paying the tarts any attention, and whining every time we passed a patch of grass. I knew the signs. He needed a toilet break.

I found a lay-by to pull into, close to a bench. I ran Meatball around the grass so he could do his business, then settled next to Louise, and we enjoyed our perfectly sweet and rich cherry cream tarts.

"Wouldn't you like a grand manor house to swan around in one day?" Louise asked.

"No. I'd be cleaning all the time and never get to enjoy it."

"You'd have staff to do that. And I hear Sir Richard is single if you want to marry into money." She waggled her eyebrows at me.

I grinned and shook my head. "You should have asked him out."

"Ha! Maybe I will. He seemed nice. A bit old for me, though. And it's a shame we only got to see the kitchen. I hoped we'd be able to poke about a bit."

"Give me a simple life over all the fanciness of a place like that." My life was good. I was happy in my job, Chef

Heston wasn't shouting at me all the time, I had Meatball, and great friends.

"By the time we get back, most of the history nerds will have gone," Louise said.

"Not yet. There's a final evening of lectures," I said. "It's an exclusive invitation only event. The Duke and Duchess arranged it for close friends and family, but I managed to sneak an invite from Princess Alice. And there's an archery contest tomorrow. That should be exciting."

"It doesn't sound all that exciting to me," Louise said. "Are we catering for the events?"

"Not tonight. But I'm making the desserts for the archery contest. I want to get there early to see people taking part. They'll be using replica longbows from medieval times. It'll be great."

She slid me a glance. "You have strange interests, Holly."

"There's nothing strange about liking history."

"What about dating? I don't see you doing much of that. Don't tell me you've given up on finding love and are only focused on stuffy history."

"Not exactly," I said. "But I already have the love of my life." I petted Meatball as he sat patiently, hoping we'd drop a few crumbs from our tarts.

"And he's a gorgeous little chap, but what about finding some delicious guy to spend your time with? I see you talking to Campbell a lot. He's yummy."

I wrinkled my nose. "I'm not interested in Campbell. Not as a boyfriend."

"He's often sneaking you off to have private chats. I think he likes you. I figured you were into him, too."

"No, he really doesn't like me. He's always telling me off. Besides, I like my men a little more geeky. You know, the bookish type. I want a man to seduce me with his brain, not his biceps."

"That's good to know," she said. "I'm tempted to ask Campbell out, but I didn't want to tread on your toes."

"Oh! Well, sure. You won't be doing that." I had a strange relationship with Campbell Milligan, the castle's head of security. Sometimes, we got along fine. Then we'd butt heads and our friendship would stall. Sometimes, it shifted into downright dislike.

"Do you know if he's dating anyone?"

"Um, he's never told me about a girlfriend. He's very private." I shrugged. "Don't you find him a bit scary? He has all those secret spy skills. What if you argued? He could make you disappear, and no one would find you."

"He's dangerous. I like that." She grinned at me. "You can guarantee you'd be protected if he took you out and you got in trouble."

"What kind of dates are you hoping he'll take you on that'll end in trouble?"

"The kind where I fall into his arms and he kisses me until I can't see straight. That's the sort of trouble I'm looking for."

I wrinkled my nose. "Campbell doesn't have a romantic bone in his body."

"I hope he's not into adventurous things that involve being outdoors." Louise's mouth twisted to the side. "I won't enjoy that. I should invite him to dinner. We could have a romantic candlelit dinner for two, and I could see if there's a soft side to Campbell."

"I've never seen one," I said. "Come on, we need to get back to the castle."

The three of us climbed back in the van. I'd only driven a short way along the road when the steering wheel tugged to the left.

I stopped as we reached the junction. "Take a look at the passenger side wheel. I'm having difficulty steering."

Louise wound down the window. "Uh oh. We've got a flat tire."

I grimaced as I pulled the van to the side of the road. We got out again and peered at the flat.

"Do you know how to change a tire?" Louise asked.

"Sure. So long as we've got the right equipment." I went to the back of the van and opened up the footwell. There was a jack, a lug wrench, and a spare tire.

I frowned as I checked the tire. It was also flat. "We have a small problem."

"No tire?"

"No air in the tire," I said.

"We'll have to ring for a rescue service."

I turned as a vehicle pulled up alongside us. It was a familiar black land cruiser used by the security teams at Audley Castle.

One window slid down, and Campbell peered out. "What are you doing here?"

I sighed. Trust him to find me when I'd gotten in difficulty. "Just dealing with the small matter of a flat tire."

A smile tracked across his face. "Don't tell me you've broken the van?"

"No! It's simply a flat. It could have happened to anyone. And I've just discovered the spare is useless. Is there any chance you can give us a tow back to the castle?"

"There's zero chance of that. Hold on. I'll sort this." Campbell reversed his vehicle behind ours. He climbed out, accompanied by two other security guards, Mason Sloane and Kace Delaney.

"It's my dream come true," Louise whispered in my ear. "We were just talking about him, and here he is. Should I ask him out now?"

"Maybe not right now," I said. "Campbell likes to compartmentalize. He has a single-track focus when he's working."

"He can have a single-track focus on me anytime he likes."

I glanced at Louise and shook my head.

Campbell walked around to the front wheel and kicked it gently. "It's flat."

"Didn't I just tell you that?" I said.

He checked over the spare tire. "This is flat as well."

I resisted the urge to tut. "Have you got something we can patch it up with?"

"Sure. Mason, get the repair kit from the trunk."

Mason nodded and headed around the back of the vehicle before returning with the repair kit.

"This is a temporary fix," Campbell said. "Don't drive any long distances or it won't hold. And when you drive back to the castle, stay below thirty miles an hour."

"That won't be a problem around here," I said.

Campbell took off his jacket and rolled up his sleeves before setting to work on repairing the tire.

"You look like you work out," Louise said.

I glanced at her and raised my eyebrows. Was she really going there, even after my warning?

"I need to keep in shape for the job," Campbell said, his attention on the tire.

"I need to get fit," Louise said. "Maybe you can give me a few pointers. Do you think I have a good figure?"

He grunted. "Holly works out a lot. Ask her. She's always trying out some weird fitness trend."

"My interest in fitness isn't weird," I said.

"You do like unusual things," Louise said. "Didn't I hear about you doing yoga with goats?"

"That was fun," I said. "And Princess Alice organized that for me."

"I'm sure you've got a few fitness tricks you can show me," Louise said to Campbell. "I'm a fast learner."

"I'm happy to hear it." He stood and nodded at the tire. "That's good to go. Mason, switch over the tires for these ladies, and we can be on our way."

"On it, boss." Mason disappeared around the side of the van with Kace.

"Thanks for helping two damsels in distress." Louise fluttered her lashes at Campbell. "We'd have been stuck if you hadn't come along."

"I'm sure we'd have figured out something," I said. "You were talking about calling for a tow truck just before Campbell arrived."

"There's no need for that," Campbell said. "This was an easy fix."

"I couldn't have done it. You're so clever," Louise said.

Campbell glanced at her, and his eyes narrowed a fraction. His attention flicked to me. "I've seen you around the history talks."

"I couldn't keep away. It was so interesting. I loved the presentation on etiquette in the royal household. And the demonstration of ancient weapons was mind blowing." I glanced at Louise. She was frowning. "Louise also likes history."

Campbell tilted his head at her. "You do?"

"Oh! Um, I mean, sure." She looked at me like I'd been speaking another language. "Why not? All those weapons and... things. Do you like history, Campbell?"

"It's not my thing."

Her shoulders slumped. Campbell wasn't making this easy on her. Louise was pretty, fun, and making it very clear she was interested in him. He wasn't picking up the hints.

"Did you see the display of weapons?" I asked. "They were authentic, discovered during several archeological digs. The lecturer said they're making replicas to test."

"It sounds riveting," Louise said, not looking at all interested as she kept staring at Campbell.

"I prefer a modern gun," Campbell said. "You don't get automatic firing and a fast reload with those ancient hunks of metal."

Of course, he would say that. "Did you hear any of the talks? The debate on the construction techniques of Kings College Chapel was interesting."

"You're being a geek," Louise whispered.

Campbell smirked. "I'll be glad when they all clear out. The extra people around means double shifts for my security team."

"Most of them will be gone by the end of the night," I said. "Then you can get back to standing around outside the family's private rooms, trying not to look bored."

"Holly!" Louise slapped my arm. "Campbell and his team do an important job protecting our employers."

Campbell grinned. "That's right. My job is crucial. Thank you for noticing."

Louise giggled. "You're most welcome."

Ugh! This was getting embarrassing. "Will you be at the shooting contest tomorrow?" I asked Campbell.

"I'll be there. Princess Alice and Lord Rupert will be attending, so security will be on hand if needed."

"You should take part in the contest," Louise said. "I bet you'd win first place."

"I would, but it's only fair to give the other contestants a chance," Campbell said.

I groaned as his huge ego made an appearance, while Louise sighed and batted her eyelashes again.

"I'm planning on getting there early to watch the action," I said. "And I've created a menu of Tudor and medieval treats for the participants to try."

"And I'll be there, too," Louise said. "You need an extra pair of hands on the day, don't you Holly?"

"I guess so. You're welcome to come along." Her offer wasn't motivated by a desire to help me. She wanted more time with Campbell.

But the man appeared immune to her flirting. His back was straight and his hands clasped behind him. Maybe he did have someone special in his life. For all I knew, he could have a secret wife tucked away.

"All finished," Mason said as he strolled back around the van with Kace.

"We'll see you back at the castle. Drive carefully." Campbell nodded and headed back to the vehicle with his colleagues before they drove away.

"He's so gorgeous." Louise climbed back in her seat and settled Meatball on her knee. "You'll have to put in a good word for me."

"Campbell never listens to anything I say." I pulled out and headed to the castle.

"You could at least find out if he's single," she said. "I don't want to waste my time chasing a man who's not available."

"I'll see what I can do," I said. "But no promises. Whenever I ask Campbell questions, he gets mean."

Louise sighed and fanned her face with a hand.

I shook my head and laughed. My thoughts briefly turned to Lord Rupert Audley. Now, he was my type. I could go for a guy like that. It was just that, I couldn't go there with him. We were friends, and I was fine with that situation. Although, sometimes, I did wonder, what would life be like being involved with Rupert?

I rolled my shoulders and concentrated on the road. I already had everything I needed to be happy. A great job, friends, and my favorite little dog by my side. I couldn't want for anything more.

Chapter 2

"I think that's everything done." I took a step back from the counter I'd been working at in the kitchen. I looked over the trays of medieval and Tudor treats I'd been working on. There were almond cakes, gingerbread, sugared almonds, and sweetmeats ready to go for tomorrow's archery contest.

I checked the time before whisking off my apron. If I didn't hurry, I'd miss the start of Professor Stephen's lecture.

I tucked the food in a chiller cabinet and washed my hands.

"Where do you think you're going, Holly?" Chef Heston yelled from across the kitchen.

"You said I could leave early," I said. "The last lecture begins in three minutes."

"Then you'll have to miss the start," he said. "Lady Philippa wants you to take some food up to her room."

Any other time, I'd have been happy to visit Lady Philippa Audley, just not today. "Can someone else do it? The topic of the talk is—"

"It could be about how to turn rocks into gold. You don't turn down an invitation from Lady Philippa." He handed me a tray of food. "Get up those stairs and go see her."

I glanced at the clock. There was no way I'd make it up the east turret, set out Lady Philippa's food, and get down in time. "I really want to see this lecture."

"And I'm sure you really want to keep your job," he said. "The first ten minutes will just be fluff and introductions. The speakers always like to talk themselves up and show how impressive they are. You can miss that and still catch the main body of the talk. But only if you stop complaining." He gave me a gentle push toward the door.

I scowled, before turning and jogging toward the east turret. I raced up the steps two at a time, charged along the corridor, and knocked on the door.

"Enter if you're handsome or rich," Lady Philippa said.

I dashed in and pulled up short. Lady Philippa wore a deep red Moroccan style gown with bell sleeves and gold embroidery. "You look beautiful. Are you going somewhere nice?"

"Holly! I'm so glad you're here." She twirled for me. "I have no plans this evening, but there's nothing wrong with wearing your finest clothing, even if no one's around to see you. Come take a seat and tell me all your news. We haven't spoken in such a long time."

"I wish I could." I set the food out as quickly as possible without appearing rude. "But I need to be somewhere."

"This sounds interesting," she said. "Or are you getting bored with my company? Is this sad, lonely old woman no longer enough for you?"

"Of course not. I love spending time with you," I said.

"So, what's the hurry? I refuse to let you leave until you answer me." She popped a cherry cream tart into her mouth.

"It's the last lecture of the history event," I said, already backing toward the door with the empty tray in my hands. "It's all about warfare and rebellion."

"That sounds fun. I'd forgotten that was going on. I thought there was some party happening that I hadn't been invited to."

"Why don't you come to the talk? You might enjoy it. Professor's Stephen's a great speaker. I've heard him talk before. He was a visiting lecturer at the university I went to." I twisted the handle of the door.

"I've never heard of him," she said. "You do make him sound intriguing, though, and I have been locked in this awful turret on my own for days. None of my terrible family have been to see me. I know they're hoping I'll turn up my toes, shuffle off this mortal coil quietly, and never bother them again."

"Lady Philippa! You know that's not true. They all love you. And you have Horatio for company. You're never alone."

"That lazy dog never gets off my bed," she said. "I do have my ghost friends to keep me company, but it's not the same. You can't hug a ghost."

I glanced over my shoulder and was glad not to see any spooky figures floating behind me. "Come to the talk with me. You'll have a great time. You may even meet Professor Stephen. He's such a clever man. He's always coming up with inventive new theories about the past. I don't know where he gets all his ideas from."

"You've convinced me." She grabbed two more cherry cream tarts. She handed me one and linked her arm through my elbow. "Let's go to this lecture."

I was careful not to hurry as we went back down the stairs, even though I was aware of the time ticking down. I didn't want to push Lady Philippa too fast and make her stumble on the uneven stone steps.

We reached the bottom of the stairs without incident and walked along the corridor. Following us at a discreet distance were two of Campbell's security team. Wherever there was a member of the Audley family, there was at least one suit clad shadow making sure they were safe.

We reached the door to the library. The room had been staged to hold the lectures during the event. It was the perfect setting with its dark wood shelving and velvet wallpaper.

"One moment please, Lady Philippa." A member of security appeared beside us. "We'll find you a suitable place to sit if you're attending the lecture."

"We'll be fine anywhere," I said.

"No, we won't. I want to be at the front. I don't want to miss a thing," Lady Philippa said.

"But we'll disturb people if we walk to the front," I said. "The talk has begun."

Her expression turned shrewd. "My sweet girl, you should take advantage of your connections. People always make room when a member of the Audley family appears. Just you watch." She patted the back of my hand.

We were waiting less than a minute before security reappeared. "Right this way, Lady Philippa." He led us past the entrance of the library.

"The talk's in here," I said, gesturing at the closed door.

He nodded and stopped by the wall next to the door. He pressed a wood panel, and a door slid open.

"Oh! The secret passages," I said. "Princess Alice showed me these not so long ago."

"They're ingenious," Lady Philippa said. "They get you in and out of almost anywhere. Lead the way," she said to her security team.

The passage was well lit and free from cobwebs as we hurried along. There was another door at the end. The security guard opened it, and after a quick look, he gestured us to go in.

Lady Philippa went first, and I followed behind. We were right at the front of the library. To my left was a temporary podium and lectern. Behind it stood the imposing figure of Professor Stephen Maguire, dressed in a smart dark suit. To my right were two hundred chairs occupied by people.

"Lady Philippa?" A young guy with round glasses and floppy dark hair that fell into his eyes approached and smiled.

"That's right," she said. "And this is my friend, Holly Holmes. We're here for the lecture."

"Of course. Your security explained everything. I'm Ben Friel, Professor Stephen's assistant. Please, come this way. We have seats for you at the front."

"That's wonderful. Thank you." She winked at me before following Ben to the seats.

The position couldn't have been better. We were right in the center of the front row.

I squirmed with excitement as I sat next to Lady Philippa and stared up at Professor Stephen.

He glanced at us, but didn't pause in delivering his lecture.

The man to my right leaned over. "Are you also a member of the Audley family?"

"No, I'm a friend of Lady Philippa's," I said. "I'm Holly."

"Nice to meet you. Johann Timber," he said softly.

I turned to stare at him. "Oh! I know you. I heard the talk you gave yesterday on the uncrowned kings of England. It was so entertaining."

He glanced at me, and a smile crossed his broad face. "Thank you. It's not every day I get told I'm entertaining."

Lady Philippa poked me with a finger, drawing my attention back to her. "I wish I'd brought snacks. Those little tarts didn't dampen my appetite. Popcorn would have been perfect."

"Try these." I pulled a small bag of sugared almonds out of my pocket.

Lady Philippa swooped the bag out of my hand as if she hadn't eaten for days and munched them as we listened to the talk.

I focused on Professor Stephen and was swiftly captivated by his warm, engaging tone as he explained the rise of rebellion and conflict during Tudor times in Britain.

I was so lucky to be here. If I didn't work at Audley Castle and wasn't friends with the family, I'd have missed all of this. It was a privilege to sit in this beautiful room and soak up some fascinating history.

The lecture was just coming to an end, when Lady Philippa squeezed my arm so hard I almost yelped.

My eyes widened when I saw her pale face. "Aren't you feeling well?"

She shook her head, her fingers clenching and unclenching. "I'm seeing... something."

I gulped and glanced around. No one else had noticed what was going on; they were still focused on Professor Stephen as he summed up his lecture.

I'd seen this behavior before from Lady Philippa. She was having a premonition, and they were rarely positive.

"Thank you for your time, ladies and gentlemen," Professor Stephen said. "I'll be around for the rest of the evening and happy to answer any questions you may have about this topic. Of course, if any of you would like copies of my new book, they're available to purchase."

The audience applauded as he stepped away from the podium.

I didn't join in. My attention was on Lady Philippa, whose lips were blue as she continued to grip my arm and gasp.

"Let's get out of here," I whispered. "Can you stand?"

She nodded, and I wrapped an arm around her waist, keeping a tight hold as I hurried her to the concealed door.

A member of security was on us in an instant. "Where are you taking Lady Philippa?"

"We need a quiet room," I said. "Lady Philippa isn't feeling well."

"I'm fine," she whispered.

"Right this way." The security guard flew into action, opening the door, hurrying us along the secret passage, into the picture gallery, and finally into a private sitting room.

Lady Philippa gasped as she collapsed on the couch and sat there panting as color slowly returned to her cheeks.

"Shall I fetch a doctor?" the security guard asked.

I turned to Lady Philippa. She was shaking her head as she struggled to sit upright.

"Do you need any help?" I asked.

She waved a hand in the air. "No, I'm fine. I had a terrible vision, though. It was awful. That lovely young man. Oh, it's so sad."

I knelt beside her and clasped her hand. "Who are you talking about?"

"Ben. The one with the round glasses we met when we arrived in the library," she said.

I glanced at the security guard, who listened intently. "What did you see?"

She sighed and shook her head. "He's going to be dead soon."

Chapter 3

"Lady Philippa, you have information about a death?" The security guard peered at her, his hand hovering by his gun holster.

I glanced at him. "It's Drayton, isn't it?" I'd seen him around the castle, but we'd never spoken. He played it even more silent and deadly than Campbell.

He nodded, his attention still fixed on Lady Philippa.

"You must have misheard." I patted her hand as I tried to figure out a way to cover for her outburst. There were only a few people who knew about her quirky ability to predict the future, and I was one of them.

Lady Philippa's breathing was rapid as her gaze locked with mine.

"My hearing is perfect," Drayton said. "Lady Philippa, I must ask, are you aware of a security breach in the castle? Is your life at risk?"

"It's not that," I said. "The family isn't at risk."

"How would you know that?" His eyes narrowed. "Did you do something to Lady Philippa?"

"Ben's going to die," Lady Philippa said. "I… I wonder if my proximity to him during the talk made the vision so strong. He's such a sweet young man. He was even answering my questions when I wasn't certain what the speaker was talking about. This is terrible news."

Drayton bristled with tension, suspicion clear on his face.

"Perhaps some tea would be good," I said. "And Lady Philippa would benefit from having Princess Alice here. Can you help with that?"

He ignored me. "Do you want me to remove this woman?"

"My name's Holly," I said. "I'm no threat. I work in the kitchen. You must have seen me around the castle."

Drayton glanced at me. "I have, but I don't know you well."

"She's fine." Lady Philippa waved him away. "I would like to see Alice, though."

There was a pause for a beat. "I'll call for backup while I find Princess Alice. Security will be right outside if you need anything." Drayton headed to the door, seeming happier now he had orders to deal with. He spoke into his comms device, which was discreetly tucked in his jacket, before leaving the room.

Lady Philippa's hands fluttered against her chest. "I should have said something to Ben. Told him to be careful."

"Tell me what you saw," I said. "How did you see Ben die?"

"The image was blurry, but I felt the life leave his body. He was on his back, outside somewhere. There were trees and leaves around him."

"Was he in the castle grounds when he died?"

"Yes, the death will be close by," she said. "Definitely on our land, and it will happen soon. That poor boy. He can't be much older than Alice."

I nodded. "Did you see how he died?"

"No. You must do something to save him." Lady Philippa clutched my hand.

"How can I help if I don't know when or how he's going to die?" I said. "Maybe he has a problem with his heart and simply collapses in the woods. I can't do anything about that."

"I can feel it in my bones. His death won't be from natural causes." She shuddered. "You can't stand by and do nothing while his life is at risk."

"I'll help if I can," I said. "But I can't walk up to the guy and warn him to look out for an unknown time and date when he'll die of an unnatural death from an unknown cause."

Lady Philippa tutted. "Don't be glib."

"I promise, I'm not. I take death seriously. Are you certain there were no more clues in your vision?"

"Granny!" Princess Alice rushed into the room, a clarinet in one hand and a music sheet in the other. She dropped them both as she landed on her knees and grabbed Lady Philippa's free hand. "I came as soon as I heard you were unwell."

"There was no need for you to worry. I'm quite well," Lady Philippa said. "I'm just having one of my funny turns."

"A funny turn that security just happened to overhear," I said. "We tried to cover things up, but didn't do a great job."

"What happened?" Alice asked, her attention fixed on Lady Philippa.

"You tell her, Holly." Lady Philippa closed her eyes.

"She thinks Professor Stephen's assistant, Ben, will be killed," I said.

Alice glanced at me as she stroked the back of Lady Philippa's hand. "We'll have none of your silliness. No one's going to die."

"My predictions are never wrong." Lady Philippa opened her eyes. "I was sitting next to the young man not ten minutes ago. We had a strong connection. He'll be dead before the week is out."

"She does seem very worried," I said. "I've never seen her have such a strong vision."

"I have." Alice adjusted her skirt around her knees. "How about a cup of hot chocolate and some marshmallows on top? That'll make you feel better. It always works for me."

"I need something stronger than hot chocolate," Lady Philippa said. "But a drink would be nice."

"Security is dealing with that," I said.

"Is Campbell helping you?" Alice's cheeks flushed, and her gaze went to the door. She was terrible at hiding the not so tiny crush she had on Campbell.

"No, it's Drayton," I said.

"Oh, well, he's capable enough." Alice turned her attention back to Lady Philippa. "There's nothing to worry about. I could play you a tune on my clarinet to distract you. Would you like that?"

"I didn't know you played the clarinet," I said.

Alice picked up the music sheet she'd dropped and placed it on the arm of the chair. "What would you like to hear, Granny?"

I tilted my head. Was she ignoring me?

Lady Philippa raised a hand. "Please, none of your clarinet. I don't think you've improved since you started learning ten years ago. Your talents lie elsewhere."

"I'd like to hear you play," I said.

Alice picked up the clarinet, but rather than playing it, she pulled off the reed and inspected it. "I can play well enough. I just don't practice as often as I should."

"You get too easily distracted," Lady Philippa said. "No one is born a genius. Everyone has to learn how to do things. Even the greatest painters didn't know one end of a brush from the other when getting started. Do you think Monet spent his time mooning over girls and not practicing?"

"Didn't he get married twice?" I asked.

"That's not helpful, Holly," Lady Philippa said.

"Some people find it easier to learn than others," Alice said.

"I'd really like to hear you play," I said. "I bet you're great."

Alice huffed out a breath as she jammed the reed back in the clarinet.

Something was definitely wrong with her, but it looked like she didn't want to share the problem with me.

Drayton returned to the room. Louise was right behind him, a tray in her hands with a pot of tea and a cup on it. Her eyes widened as she saw me sitting with Lady Philippa, but she didn't comment as she poured the tea and handed Lady Philippa the cup.

"Thank you, my dear," Lady Philippa said. Her hands shook a little as she took a sip. "I'm already feeling much better. There's no need for all this fuss. As soon as I left the library, I began to recover."

"You shouldn't have been at the lecture," Alice said. "The doctor has told you lots of times not to get stressed. It's bad for your nerves."

Louise took the empty tray and left the room, but I could tell she was dying to question me about what was going on.

"Can I get you anything else?" Drayton hovered close by.

"Thank you, no. I just need some quiet," Lady Philippa said.

He nodded before heading to the door and closing it behind him.

"It was a talk on warfare," I said to Alice. "Maybe that didn't help."

Alice shrugged. "It sounds boring."

What was going on with her? "You like history. You've been researching your family tree for ages."

She shot me another glance but didn't reply.

"It was a good talk," Lady Philippa said. "I was enjoying myself. Then I got this strange burning inside me."

"Are you sure you're not coming down with a water infection?" Alice asked.

"For goodness sake. Not a burning sensation down there!" Lady Philippa's expression turned sharp. "I know when I'm having a premonition. It didn't help that I had nothing to write it down on. I had to sit there and experience the full force of it, and right next to the victim."

I rubbed my wrist. Lady Philippa had held onto me so tightly, I was sure I'd have bruises in the morning. "It's over now. There's nothing to worry about."

She shook her head. "But there is. You must watch over Ben."

I looked at Alice, but she made a point of not meeting my gaze. "I'll do what I can, but I can hardly follow him around all day. Maybe we could get security to watch over him if you really think he's in danger."

"That won't work. Campbell is always polite around me, but he believes I'm an eccentric old woman with an overactive imagination," Lady Philippa said. "If we try to get him to tail Ben because I've seen that he's going to die, he won't believe me. It has to be you, Holly. You have a friendly way about you. Dazzle him with your treats and try to keep him out of harm's way."

"And make yourself another new friend while you're at it," Alice said.

"A new friend? What are you talking about?" I asked.

"You know what I'm talking about," Alice said. "I shouldn't have to explain myself to you."

The anger in her voice was clear, but I had no idea what I'd done to offend her. Had I overstepped the line, somehow? I always tried to be careful when it came to our friendship. I was only too aware that we moved in different social circles, but Alice never seemed bothered by that. In fact, when I'd asked her about it not long after we'd become friends, she'd laughed and told me not to be silly. Had I made a huge social faux pas I wasn't aware of, and she was embarrassed to be seen talking to me?

My stomach churned as I tried to figure out what I'd done wrong.

"Holly, promise me you'll watch over Ben." Lady Philippa caught hold of my hand and squeezed.

"She won't have time for that," Alice said.

"I'll do what I can, but Alice is right, I will be busy in the kitchen."

"I wasn't talking about your work," Alice said. "You'll be too busy with your new best friend to worry about Ben."

Alice was acting jealous. Why did she think I had a new best friend? "Who are you talking about?"

She hopped to her feet and grabbed her clarinet. "As if you don't know. Now, if you'll excuse me. I need to practice so my playing doesn't offend anyone." She stomped out of the room.

I winced as the door slammed shut.

"It looks like you've hurt her feelings," Lady Philippa said.

I stared at the door. "It does. I don't get it. Alice is jealous because I have other friends?"

"Of course. She's worried you're replacing her with somebody else. Isn't that obvious?"

"I'd never do that. I value my friendship with Alice. She's one-of-a-kind. I wouldn't change a thing about her."

"You need to tell her that," Lady Philippa said. "Alice may be a princess, but that doesn't mean she's immune to worry. She's feeling threatened by someone in your life."

"Who?"

"That's for you to find out." She let out a sigh. "I'm feeling better now I have my premonition out in the open. Call security, and I'll have them return me to my turret. This has been quite an adventure. Thank you so much for inviting me to the lecture."

"I'm not sure I deserve your thanks after what happened."

"You do. It's good to get the blood racing now and again. Go get that stern-faced young man in here."

I stood, hurried to the door, and informed Drayton that Lady Philippa was ready to go.

I waited as he escorted her away. My mind was full of Ben's upcoming murder, how I could stop it, and how to make things up to Alice when I wasn't certain what I'd even done wrong.

This had been a strange day. And I had a feeling that things were about to get even stranger if Lady Philippa's prediction came true.

Chapter 4

It had only just gone six o'clock in the morning, and I was jogging past the main castle exit for the twelfth time.

Meatball bounced along next to me, excited to be out so early, so he could sniff the fascinating morning smells and chase after birds as they hunted for a tasty breakfast.

I'd barely slept the previous night, thinking up ways to watch over Ben without it looking peculiar. I'd decided an extended jogging session was in order.

Jogging wasn't my favorite past-time when it came to keeping fit, but it got me outside the castle, and I could cover large distances while I kept an eye out for Ben.

I'd noticed that he'd taken a walk before breakfast each morning, and I wanted to make sure I didn't miss him. Maybe it would be on this morning walk that he'd meet a sticky end.

I rested my hands on my knees and sucked in a few deep breaths. I couldn't stay out much longer or it would start to look odd. Plus, my legs felt like jelly. I'd been jogging backward and forward pass the main exit for almost an hour. I couldn't have missed him, could I?

My gaze went to the trees in the near distance. What if he was already dead? There were numerous exits out of the castle. He could have changed his route this morning, and I'd been lurking around the wrong place.

I stepped toward the trees but then stopped. The woods were too big to search on my own. There were acres of trees around the castle grounds. I'd jog for another ten minutes, then head inside and lurk around the private dining quarters to see if Ben came down for breakfast.

"I've already told you, I'm not interested." A petite redhead wearing black dungarees and boots hurried out the door. Her hair was piled on top of her head in a messy bun and her cheeks were bright pink.

"Don't be like that, gorgeous. What's the harm in having a bit of fun?" A tall stocky guy, with dark stubble on his chin and tattoos peeking over the collar of his T-shirt, strolled out behind her, a smug smile on his face. He was roguishly handsome but looked like trouble through and through.

The woman glanced over her shoulder at him. "Please, just leave me alone."

"You were all smiles and giggles yesterday," the man said. "What's changed?"

"I was just being friendly. There's no harm in that. I didn't expect you to get the wrong idea."

I jogged along at a safe distance behind them. It sounded like a lover's quarrel, so I didn't want to interfere. They must be involved with the history conference.

"You're breaking my heart." The man caught hold of the woman's arm and yanked her around toward him. "A kiss and a cuddle, that's all I'm after. No ties. We can both go our separate ways at the end of the day. No one else needs to know, if you're worried about sullying that innocent act you've got going on."

The woman gasped and shoved her hands against his broad chest. "I said no. You need to back off."

The man pulled her closer and lowered his head as if he was about to kiss her.

Meatball raced over and began to bark, bouncing around them and growling. He could always sense trouble, and it was radiating off that guy like he wore it as a heady cologne.

"Get out of here." The man dropped his hold on the woman as he shooed Meatball away.

I jogged over. "Is everything okay? I hope my dog's not bothering you. He's safe. He just gets excited when he meets new people."

The man's green gaze met mine, and he scowled. "He is bothering me. Get lost, both of you."

The woman's wide eyes met mine, and she shook her head. She needed my help.

"We've not met. I'm Holly. I work at the castle." I held out my hand to the woman and tried a reassuring smile on her, hoping to convey that I had no plans to go anywhere while this guy was hassling her.

She grabbed my hand and held on tight, her smile wavering. "Penny Brentwood. I'm with the history event."

"Nice to meet you, Penny." I dropped her hand and turned my attention to the man who radiated trouble. "And you are?"

"Getting out of here." He shot a glare at Penny before turning and striding back into the castle.

Penny let out a sigh of relief. "Thank you so much for coming to my rescue."

"You should be thanking Meatball," I said. "He must have sensed there was a problem. He's good like that. He's very intuitive around people. I take it that guy isn't your boyfriend."

"No, thank goodness. That was Eddie. He's one of the tech hands working at the history event. He sets up the lighting rigs and staging. He noticed me on the first day and has been pestering me ever since."

"He's not your type?" I asked.

Penny bent and petted Meatball on the head, who happily accepted the fuss. "I've already found my type. My boyfriend, Ben, is a part of the history conference, too."

"Ben Friel? I met him last night at the talk Professor Stephen gave," I said. This was a perfect opportunity to find out more about Ben. If I could learn his movements, I may be able to steer him away from his untimely demise.

She smiled up at me. "That's right. He's been working so hard at this conference."

"It's been an amazing event. I haven't managed to attend all the talks, but the ones I've heard were fascinating."

"That's good to know." Penny stood from petting Meatball. "The stress has been keeping Ben awake at night. He's so jumpy. I've been encouraging him to get out and take a long walk before everything kicks off each day. I think it's helping, but I don't know, though."

"How did you meet?" I asked.

"At university," she said. "I'm in my second year of a history PhD. Ben's in his final year and has been assisting Professor Stephen for the last six months."

"I admire Professor Stephen's work," I said. "I also studied history at university. I've seen him talk several times."

Penny nodded. "He's a clever man, even more so since he picked Ben to assist him. Don't tell anyone I said this, but I reckon Ben's even cleverer than Professor Stephen. He's already making a name for himself and has had three papers published in academic journals. I'm so proud of him."

"Have you mentioned Eddie's unwanted attention to Ben?" I asked. Maybe Eddie would go after Ben if he wanted his woman.

"No. And I can usually handle myself with guys," she said. "It's just that Eddie's extremely persistent. He's asked me out a dozen times. When I said I wasn't interested, he moved on to suggesting we simply hook up. That's not what I do."

"Some guys don't like to accept they're not a super stud to all women."

"You're right about that. But I'd never worry Ben with something so trivial." Penny shrugged. "Besides, he's more of an armchair debater than a fighter. I can't imagine him getting in a physical fight, and I wouldn't want him to fight over me."

"I'm certain he'd want to make sure you were safe," I said. "If Eddie is threatening you, we can speak to the castle security. They can have him removed."

"No! That'll only add to Ben's stress. Unfortunately, Eddie is great at his job. If he's made to leave, they'll be down a tech hand." She shook her head. "Thanks, but I'll be okay. And this is the last day. We've just got the shooting contest later, and then we're heading off. Besides, Eddie will be busy most of the day disassembling the rigging and equipment. That should keep him distracted long enough to keep his hands off me and his mind on the job."

"If you're sure," I said.

She nodded, her smile looking strained. "Positive."

"You mentioned Ben's been stressed recently," I said. "Is it just about this event, or is something else troubling him?"

"I, um, I'm not sure what you mean," Penny said.

"I used to get stressed when I had assignments due," I said. "Could that be what's worrying him?"

"Oh! Possibly. He's always busy with his work. He's working on a paper about a recent archeological find. It could revolutionize academic thinking when it comes to building construction methods in the early Tudor period. He's excited about it, but I know he's finding it stressful. Academics can be a stuffy lot and slow to change. This new find will put a few people's noses out of joint."

I stepped closer, my inner history geek interested. "What was the find?"

She bit her bottom lip and shook her head. "I only know the basics. Ben is planning a book based on the excavation, and it's keeping him crazy busy. We don't get to spend as much time together as I'd like. Still, I shouldn't complain. We're doing what we love."

"Do you help him with his research?"

"No, we specialize in different historical periods. Once we're both finished with our studies, I'm hoping we can find jobs in the same city."

"You're both staying in academia?"

"I hope so. Ben is guaranteed a job, but I may struggle to find something suitable. I'm hoping to teach history if I can't get a place at a university to lecture."

"It sounds like you have big plans."

"I do. And Ben, well, he's always focused on his research and the past." She gave a wry smile. "Trust me to fall in love with a brainiac."

"I'll have to get a copy of Ben's book when it comes out," I said.

"I'll tell him you said that. He'll be thrilled." Her smile faded. "Look out. Smug jerk alert."

I turned and spotted a tall thin guy with slicked back dark hair coming toward us. He looked about the same age as Penny and wore an aging leather jacket and jeans. "Do you know him?"

"I do." She sighed and shook her head. "Marcel is trying to be the Indiana Jones of the history world. He even has the same style hat that the actor wore in the movies."

He stopped walking and nodded at us. "Good morning, Penny. And you, I don't know." His gaze settled on me.

"I'm Holly Holmes," I said. "I was just talking to Penny about Ben's work."

"Marcel Miles." His top lip curled. "Bragging about your wonder boyfriend again, Penny. You should know, the last academic paper he published had an error. I reported the problem to the Historical Council."

"No, it didn't," Penny said. "You keep saying that, but Ben triple checks his sources. Everything was fine. You have sour grapes because his paper got selected instead of yours."

Marcel pulled back his shoulders and jutted out his chin. "I'll have you know, I've had several requests to see that paper. It'll be peer reviewed and published by the end of the year. And it won't have a single mistake in it."

"Good luck with that," Penny said.

"I don't need luck. My research speaks for itself," Marcel said. "Anyway, where is Ben?"

"He left early this morning," Penny said. "He had a package to pick up and then planned to take a walk around the village."

I groaned inwardly. My early morning start had been for nothing. I'd missed Ben. And he wasn't in mortal danger; he was taking a fun stroll around Audley St. Mary and soaking up the village's history.

"I need to talk to him about that funding proposal," Marcel said. "When will he be back?"

"I'm his girlfriend, not his keeper," Penny said. "But I expect him back in time for breakfast. You know what he's like, though. He gets distracted. It could be noon before he puts in an appearance."

"He'd better not be late for the shooting competition," Marcel said. "I've got an excellent replica longbow I plan to beat him with."

"I'm looking forward to the competition," I said. "Will you all be there?"

Marcel's gaze ran over me. "You shoot?"

"No, but I wouldn't mind watching other people have a go. I'll be bringing out refreshments halfway through the event."

"You work at the castle?" Marcel said.

"That's right. In the kitchen. I specialize in making the desserts for the café and the family."

He took a step back. "You're a sandwich maker?"

My fingers flexed and my smile stiffened. "No, I'm trained in making high-quality desserts."

"Did you make that amazing gingerbread that was served the first night we were here?" Penny asked.

I smiled at her and nodded. "I used an original Tudor recipe. The Audley family has a library crammed full of incredible texts, including some first edition cookery books dating back hundreds of years. They're a joy to look through. I love trying the recipes in them."

"The Audley family let you use their library?" The disbelief in Marcel's voice was clear.

"Don't be such a snob," Penny said. "That gingerbread was out of this world. I usually find modern desserts too sweet, but that was perfect. The ginger almost blew my head off."

"That's exactly how it's supposed to taste," I said.

"Any chance you can give me the recipe? I'd love to make it for Ben. He missed out on the desserts that night," Penny said.

"Of course," I said. "And I'm glad you enjoyed it. There'll be more today at the competition."

Marcel tutted. "I'm sure your desserts taste nothing like those served in Tudor times. That's just untrained speculation."

"Marcel, don't be rude. And unless you have a time machine and can go back to that period and try the desserts, you're not able to substantiate that statement either," Penny said.

"Neither is she." He jutted out his chin again, a petulant look on his face.

Penny shared a glance with me. "All I know, is the desserts Holly made were incredible."

I smiled smugly at Marcel. "Thanks. I appreciate that."

Penny winked at me. "Any time."

"I can't hang around here if you're going to gossip about recipes," Marcel said. "I've had an exclusive invitation to go to breakfast with Professor Stephen and Evelyn. I can't keep them waiting. When you see that useless boyfriend of yours, tell him I'm looking for him." Marcel didn't even spare me a glance as he turned and walked away.

Penny shook her head. "Marcel is a nightmare. He's so jealous of Ben."

"Is Marcel also helping with the conference?" I asked.

"Yes, he's another of Professor Stephen's assistants," she said. "He takes on two assistants every year because he has so much work. Ben's his number one. He always gets the best jobs. Marcel is left to pick over the scraps and do the boring work. He hates Ben because of that. In fact, he has a chip on his shoulder about just about everything."

That was an interesting motive for murder. If Ben died, Marcel would step into his shoes and become number one assistant to Professor Stephen. I mentally tucked away that information.

"I'd better not keep you," I said. "Enjoy the shooting competition today."

"Thanks, I will. I hope to see you there. And I'll definitely sample your desserts." Penny touched my arm. "Ignore what Marcel said about them. The man lives off instant noodles and takeout. He wouldn't know a good meal if it landed in his mouth."

I laughed before saying goodbye and heading back to my apartment with Meatball. I needed a shower before I started work.

I had several interesting pieces of information about Ben, but couldn't do anything with them, not yet. As far as I knew, Ben was still alive and kicking. The mystery of who might kill Ben Friel was still ongoing.

Chapter 5

"Hurry up, Holly." Chef Heston glared at me as I stacked the last tray of treats on the trolley to take to the shooting competition.

I grumbled under my breath. I'd planned to get to the competition early so I could see the contestants taking part, but the industrial mixer had broken, and a kitchen assistant had cut her thumb so badly she'd needed to go to the hospital. That left all of us scrambling to play catch up and get the food ready for the hungry visitors in the café.

"I'll come with you, Holly." Louise bounded over and winked at me. "You said you needed a hand, didn't you?"

"No, you stay here," Chef Heston said. "There are two vats of soup that need to be watched and a dozen loaves of bread to come out of the oven in twenty minutes."

"But… but… Holly said I could go with her," Louise said.

"Who's in charge of this kitchen?" Chef Heston snapped.

"You are, Chef." Louise lowered her head.

"Which means, you follow my orders, not Miss Holmes'," he said. "Now, snap to it, both of you. Louise, you're on soup and bread duty. Holly, take those desserts to the shooting party, and be quick about it. No lingering."

"As if I'd ever linger," I said.

He waved a spatula at me. "Out. Now."

I shrugged an apology at Louise as I hurried past. An extra pair of hands would have been nice, but I knew her reason for wanting to come with me. It had nothing to do with food, and everything to do with getting a chance to flirt with Campbell.

A quiet whistle from me once I was outside had Meatball racing out of his kennel. He bounced around the trolley and danced on his back legs.

"I know, it's exciting. We're getting an extra walk today. Do you want to see the shooting?"

"Woof, woof!" He gave a whole body wiggle before racing off in front of me, his tail up and his ears pricked.

I bumped the trolley along the path, being careful to avoid any dips as I headed onto the grass toward the shooting range.

The range was located a short distance from the castle, set among a clearing in the woods.

I grinned and sped up as voices filtered toward me. Maybe I'd still have a chance to see the contestants in action.

"Holly, wait up."

I turned and smiled as Rupert jogged toward me. In one hand he held a longbow.

"I thought you'd already be at the contest," I said.

"I needed to head back to the castle for a few minutes. I'm glad to see you, and all that lovely food. All this exercise works up an appetite." He pushed his messy blond hair off his forehead.

"All of this was made to authentic instructions from an ancient recipe book I discovered in your library."

"It looks delicious. Let me help with the trolley."

"You don't have to do that," I said. "You've got your bow."

"You take that, I'll push." He held out the bow.

I sucked in a breath as I studied it. "It's beautiful." The wood was polished to a dark glossy brown.

He grinned. "Isn't it? I had a man who works using medieval design techniques create it for me. You're holding a piece of living history."

I stroked my fingers over the polished wood. "There are engravings on it."

"It's the family motto," he said. "I got one made for Alice as well."

"Oh, of course. Alice will be shooting." My smile slipped. Would she still be angry with me?

"She's not supposed to be here," he said. "We're using medieval tournament rules. That means, no women allowed. Typical Alice, she doesn't listen to a word I say. We've all told her she can't take part, but she joined in, anyway." Rupert pushed the trolley slowly in front of him. "The embarrassing thing is, she's trouncing us all. If we were really in Tudor times, she'd have been burned at the stake for being so good at shooting. Everyone would have believed she was using dark magic. Women aren't supposed to be skilled with longbows."

"Good for her. I'm glad she's doing well." Maybe Alice had forgiven me by now, especially if she was in a good mood because she was winning this contest.

"Is everything okay?" Rupert asked. "You and Alice haven't had a falling out? I mentioned your name earlier, and she went quiet just like you did."

"No, everything's fine," I said. "I'm looking forward to seeing the shooting."

"It should be my turn by the time we get there," he said. "I'm in third place. I hope to get at least a second."

"I'm sure you'll do well," I said. "How's everyone else doing?"

"Not bad. Professor Stephen is a bit of a braggart, though. He keeps saying he's got thirty years' experience of shooting ancient weapons, but he hasn't hit the bullseye once. His colleague, Johann, is awful." Rupert leaned closer. "And he keeps taking sneaky sips from a hip flask in his pocket. He thinks nobody is noticing, but the fact his aim is so wildly off, it would be hard to miss that something's not right with him. I don't think he's hit the target the last five times he's shot. Everyone else is a half-decent shot."

Meatball raced out of the trees, barking when he saw us, before speeding off.

We walked into the trees and along a flat path which widened into the clearing being used for the shooting contest.

Campbell and Drayton stood off to one side. In the distance were four large round targets set against a bank of mud and sand bags.

"That was my lucky arrow that shot over the top of that last target," Johann said.

"It's not about luck. It's about aiming correctly." Ben stood next to him, an amused smile on his face as he listened to Johann. Penny was also with them, looking around the site. She seemed a little bored.

Marcel stood off to one side with Professor Stephen and a woman I didn't recognize, but from how closely she stood next to him, I had to assume she was his wife.

Alice faced the targets, an arrow notched and her attention on the shooting range.

My breath caught, and I stopped walking as she let the arrow fly. It sailed through the air and slammed into the middle of the target.

I clapped before I could stop myself. "Well done, Princess Alice. That was brilliant."

Alice lowered her bow and turned. Our gazes met before she looked away.

My smile faded. It seemed I still had work to do to win her friendship back. I frowned and focused on setting out the food. Maybe I shouldn't work on the friendship. Alice was the jealous one. She needed to get over it. I wasn't replacing her just because I had another friend. It was unfair to expect me to have her as a friend and no one else.

Meatball bounded into the clearing and trotted over to me. He raised a paw, cutely begging for a treat.

I checked no one was watching before taking a scone and feeding him a piece, then pocketed the rest.

Rupert swiped a piece of gingerbread. "Your scores still don't count, Alice. No matter how many times you hit the bullseye."

"They absolutely do count." Alice marched over and glared at him. "Times have changed. Women can shoot, too. And, as I'm demonstrating, a lot better than anyone else here."

"We're still following the medieval rules of a longbow contest," Rupert said.

She smacked him on the back of the head with an arrow shaft. "These are the revised rules. Don't you think, Holly?"

I lifted my eyebrows. She was talking to me now? "I don't know enough about archery to have any useful input."

Alice's lips pursed before her attention turned to the food. "Is that almond cake?"

"That's right," I said. "Why don't you try some?"

Her hand hesitated in the air for a second before she grabbed a cake and bit into it. "It's delicious."

"Excuse me a moment, ladies. I need to talk to Professor Stephen." Rupert strolled away.

I focused on rearranging the already neat trays of food. "Are you enjoying the contest?"

"It's good," Alice said through a mouthful of cake. "But the boys are being so annoying, claiming that my scores don't count."

"You're a great shot," I said. "I'd probably accidentally shoot myself if I tried using a longbow."

"No, you wouldn't. It's all in the technique," she said.

"You'll have to show me some time." I lifted my head and met her gaze. "Especially now you're talking to me again. Are you still angry with me?"

Her eyes narrowed as she finished her cake. "I don't know what you're talking about."

"Yesterday, when I helped Lady Philippa, you were being mean to me."

"I... well, there may have been a misunderstanding." She scraped a foot through some fallen leaves.

"Which one of us misunderstood, and what did we mistake?"

She huffed out some air. "I saw you out for the day with your friend from the kitchen. And... I got jealous." She grabbed another cake and stuffed it into her mouth.

I touched her arm. "Alice, I can be friends with lots of people. That doesn't mean I like you any less."

She waved a hand in the air as she chewed. "I know that. But ever since you've been here, I've felt happier. I can't explain it. I can be myself around you, and you don't think I'm silly or pointless."

"Anyone who tells you you're either of those things isn't worth associating with. No matter how many fancy titles or manor houses they own," I said. "Alice, you're brilliant. I love having you as a friend."

She flung her arms around me, making me squeak because she squeezed so hard. "You're my best friend," she whispered in my ear, her breath smelling of sweet almonds and sugar.

I laughed and hugged her back. "And if you don't mind coming second to Meatball, you're my best friend, too."

"I can handle that. Meatball is adorable." She stepped back and grinned at me before giving Meatball a brief pat. "I didn't mean to be petty and make you feel bad. You can have other friends, just so long as you remember that I'm the best friend you'll ever have. Well, the best friend without fur and a tail that you'll ever have."

"I could never forget that," I said.

"And, I promise, I'll make it up to you," she said.

"There's no need to do that. I'm just relieved we're talking again. It felt weird when you ignored me."

"I have to make amends. And I know just how to do it." She grinned at me. "You'll love it."

I bit my bottom lip. Sometimes, Alice's surprises were on the eccentric side, but I wasn't turning down her olive branch. "I look forward to it. How's Lady Philippa doing? She had a shock yesterday when she had that vision."

"She seemed better when I checked on her in the evening," Alice said. "She was having a hot chocolate and talking to the wall as if somebody was in the room with her, so pretty much back to normal."

I looked over at Ben, who was still chatting to Johann. "Did she say anything more about her prediction? She said Ben would die close to some trees, and we're surrounded by them."

"It won't happen here," she said. "We've got security on hand. Everyone will see if someone runs out and shoots Ben."

"Did Lady Philippa tell you a gun would be used to kill him?"

"No, she's never that helpful when it comes to her strange little visions," Alice said. "But he's been fine ever since we got here. He's not a bad shot, either."

"Five minutes until the next round begins," Rupert called. "Before we start, please help yourself to the delicious treats prepared by our kitchen. They're made from authentic medieval recipes. I can assure you they're wonderful." He looked over at me and smiled.

The next few minutes kept me busy as I handed out cakes to the hungry contestants.

I was surprised to see Eddie jog out of the trees with a handful of arrows and place them down before disappearing back into the woods.

"What's he doing here?" I asked Alice, nodding at Eddie.

"We needed someone to grab our arrows in between rounds," Alice said. "That guy overheard us talking when we were standing outside the castle and volunteered to help."

"That's surprisingly nice of him," I said, my gaze drifting to Penny.

Alice arched an eyebrow. "Do you know him?"

"Not really. I saw him this morning hassling Penny, Ben's girlfriend. He wasn't taking no for an answer and didn't back off until Meatball chased him away."

"He's been behaving himself so far," Alice said. "Although now you mention it, he has been spending time hanging around Penny when he has nothing to do. I hope he's not causing her problems. I can send him away and get one of the boys to do the hard work of arrow hunting. Unless you want a job."

"No way! I don't want to hunt in the dirt for your arrows." I shook my head. "Just keep an eye on him. Make sure he's not a problem for Penny. I don't want her to feel threatened by him."

"He won't get anywhere near her when I'm around," Alice said. "If he hassles her, I'll set Campbell on him. No! I'll shoot him."

I chuckled. "Maybe don't shoot anyone. Even a princess can get in trouble for doing that."

"It would be a non-lethal shot. Maybe through the calf or the upper arm. Somewhere he wouldn't bleed out right away."

I shuddered. Sometimes Alice had a dark sense of humor.

"If everybody's ready, I believe Professor Stephen's next to shoot," Rupert said.

The contestants collected their longbows and arrows, and Professor Stephen strode up to the mark.

"He's not all that good," Alice whispered. "He over-stretches his bow string. It'll snap if he's not careful, and he'll have to withdraw from the contest. You're only allowed one weapon per round."

Professor Stephen notched his arrow, lined up his shot, and let the arrow fly. It was a solid try, and it landed just outside the main bullseye.

"Is that his wife?" I asked as the slim middle-aged blonde I'd seen him standing with clapped.

"That's right. Evelyn Maguire. She comes with him when he does his lectures. I think she's involved with the private functions he hosts. She's nice. Very friendly. She doesn't know much about history, though. And she doesn't shoot."

"I bet you can't make the bullseye this time," Johann said to Professor Stephen. "You're five points behind Alice, so you need a high score."

"Her points don't count." Professor Stephen didn't turn as he notched his next arrow. "No offense, Princess."

"They do count," Alice muttered. "And I am offended. Even if they don't declare me the winner, we'll know the truth. We'll celebrate later with some of those delicious cherry cream pies I've seen in the kitchen."

I smiled at her. "Absolutely. You'll beat all these show-offs."

Professor Stephen lined up his next shot. He raised his arm and sighted along the arrow shaft.

"Do you see what I mean about his poor technique?" Alice whispered.

I didn't, not really, but I nodded along, happy to watch the contest.

Professor Stephen let out a grunt and dropped his longbow. His hand went to his back, and he leaned forward.

"Darling, what's wrong?" Evelyn rushed over and caught hold of his arm.

"Aargh! My wretched back. I think a muscle just popped." He grimaced as he tried to straighten, then shook his head and remained hunched over. "I can't move."

"That's because of his bad technique," Alice said to me. "If you have a weak core, and don't hold yourself properly, you get hurt. Combine that with his over-reach, and this was bound to happen."

"We'd better go and see if he's okay."

We walked over and joined the rest of the group who surrounded Professor Stephen and Evelyn.

"You're going to have to withdraw, old boy." Johann sounded pleased by the prospect.

"Of course I will. I can hardly shoot in this condition," Professor Stephen said through gritted teeth.

"So, you're forfeiting?" Johann looked around the group, a big smile on his face. His cheeks were glowing, and I doubted it was because of the exercise he'd been getting during this contest.

"Even though I'll have to give up, you still won't get a place in the winners' row," Professor Stephen said. "Your last shots didn't hit the target. It's time you got your eyes checked."

Johann chuckled. "I have twenty-twenty vision."

"It's not his vision that's the problem," Alice whispered in my ear. "He's drained two hip flasks, and they weren't full of apple juice, not from the smell on his breath."

"Is there anything I can get you, Professor Stephen?" Marcel nudged past Ben to stand beside him. "Pain medication? Or a hot compress for your back?"

"No, I just need to rest," Professor Stephen said. "Evelyn, help me back to the castle. I need to lie down."

"Of course." She looked over at Rupert. "Is there a shortcut to the castle from here? A long walk won't be any good for his back."

"Yes. Go straight past the shooting range. It's a little overgrown, but it'll cut ten minutes off the walk. You'll see the castle in front of you once you get around the corner."

"Thank you," she said. "Come on, darling. Let's get you into bed."

"Better luck next time," Johann said. He turned to Marcel. "Where's that guy with our arrows? It's my turn to shoot, and my lucky arrow isn't in that pile over there."

"I haven't seen him," Marcel said.

"I'd better go and get it. Come help me look, Marcel."

Marcel frowned, his attention on Professor Stephen. "Are you sure I can't help you?"

Professor Stephen waved him away. "Go with Johann. He needs all the help he can get to find that arrow."

"Very well." Marcel frowned, clearly not happy at being dismissed.

"Can we pause things for a few minutes?" Johann looked over at Rupert.

"That's fine," Rupert said. "We won't be able to shoot until Professor Stephen and Evelyn are clear of the shooting range. Everyone take five minutes."

Johann and Marcel headed off into the trees to hunt for the arrow, while I walked back to the food trolley and waited with Alice and Rupert, watching and wincing as Professor Stephen limped away with his wife.

"I bet he's disappointed he can't finish the contest," I said.

She pursed her lips. "Maybe he faked his injury."

"Alice, that's not a nice thing to say," Rupert said. "Why would he do that?"

"He was losing," she said. "Professor Stephen got desperate and pretended to hurt his back so he wouldn't have to concede to a girl. Imagine the shame if that happened." She giggled and winked at me.

"Yes, we all know how amazing you are," Rupert said. "But you could be a little more charitable to our visiting expert. It won't do his reputation any good to know he was beaten by you."

"Which is why he faked his injury." Alice grinned at me. "You agree, don't you Holly?"

"I, um, he did seem in a lot of pain. That's hard to fake."

Ben walked over with Penny by his side. "I believe we have you to thank for the delicious food." His smile was warm as he nodded at me.

"It was my pleasure," I said, noticing several marks on Ben's face. They looked like bruises. "Have you enjoyed your time here?"

"It's been great," he said. "I've loved getting a behind-the-scenes look at the castle."

Penny's phone rang, and she pulled it out of her pocket. "Excuse me a moment. I need to take this." She wandered away from the group and disappeared into the trees.

"Your longbow is incredible, Princess Alice," Ben said.

"Rupert had this custom-made for me," she said. "I have three more. All unique designs, but this is my favorite. It shoots perfectly straight."

"It's an impressive piece of craftsmanship," Ben said.

"Do you want to try it?"

"Are you serious?" Ben's smile widened, his gaze hungry as he stared at her bow.

"Of course. Come on, you can get a feel for it while we wait for the all clear to start shooting." She led Ben away and handed him her longbow.

I glanced over at Campbell and Drayton, who stood statue still. Nothing seemed out of place here. Maybe Lady Philippa's prediction about Ben's demise wouldn't come true today. Everyone was relaxed and happy as they chatted and finished the food.

I took a plate of treats to Campbell and Drayton. "Would you like to try some of these?"

Drayton nodded and selected an almond cake. "Thanks."

Campbell didn't move.

"Would you like a cake, Campbell?" I waved the plate under his nose.

"No. Go away. We're on duty."

I lowered the plate. That was just rude. I was only being friendly.

"Sorry about the misunderstanding with Lady Philippa," Drayton said.

"No problem. I hope you now realize I'm no threat. I'm all about the baking."

Drayton glanced at Campbell. "Yep. I've been told all about you."

My eyes narrowed as I glared at Campbell. I could imagine all the uncomplimentary things he'd said about me.

"I heard you had trouble with the work van," Drayton said. "Did everything get sorted?"

"Almost. It's getting new tires," I said. "Although Chef Heston wasn't happy about it, he could hardly blame me about the flat tires, especially not the spare. I had nothing to do with that."

Campbell grunted.

"Isn't that right?" I shoved the plate up to his nose again. He was in a bad mood today. "Are you sure you don't want a cake?"

"Go on, boss," Drayton said. "One won't hurt. They're delicious."

"Holly, you're blocking my line of sight," Campbell said.

I turned and walked away. I couldn't understand what Louise saw in him. He was far too grumpy to be a good boyfriend.

Alice was still chatting with Ben and showing him her longbow, while everyone else hung around waiting for Johann and Marcel to get back from their arrow hunt.

I placed the plate down and checked over the remaining food. As much as I wanted to, I couldn't stay here, or Chef Heston would yell at me for slacking off. But I also didn't want to leave Ben, not while there was a chance he could get hurt.

Alice walked over and tucked a hand through my elbow. "Isn't this fun?"

"It's great," I said. "How much longer will the contest go on?"

"We've got another five rounds," she said. "We'll be out here for at least an hour."

I couldn't wait around all that time. "You haven't seen anything suspicious in regard to Ben? He's not had an argument with someone, or you've spotted anyone being mean to him?"

"No! Holly, you're worrying about nothing. And Campbell is here if anything happens."

Meatball appeared and raced around the clearing, stopping for a welcome pat now and again. He bounded over to Campbell and stood in front of him, wagging his tail, his paw raised.

Drayton went to pet him, but a sharp word from Campbell stopped him and he stood straight again.

That was mean. Campbell must have gotten out of the wrong side of the bed today. All Meatball wanted was a little pet and to be told he was a good boy.

"Meatball, come here." I patted my knee, and he bounced over.

I knelt to give him some more scone and a belly rub.

A blur of movement caught my eye, closely followed by another. I turned my head to see what it was.

Ben yelped, dropped the longbow he held, and staggered backward.

I stood, my heart thundering in my chest. I was about to race over to Ben, when Campbell shot past me like a bullet out of a gun.

I hurried after him, my eyes widening as I took in the scene. Ben was flat on his back, his arms splayed, and an arrow sticking out of his chest.

Chapter 6

"Everybody stay calm. Remain in a group," Campbell ordered, his gaze scanning the trees.

I stared down at Ben, feeling winded as shock coursed through me. "Is he…"

Campbell glanced up as he felt for a pulse in Ben's neck. "He's dead."

My breath rushed out of me. I felt guilty, even though I'd had nothing to do with his death. Lady Philippa had predicted this, and she'd told me to look out for Ben.

"Drayton, search the woods. There's a shooter out there. The arrow came from that direction." Campbell pointed behind the shooting range.

"I'm on it." Drayton sprinted into the woods, his gun drawn.

Campbell stood and spoke into his comms device. "Alpha team two, we have a situation at the shooting range. Six men to dispatch to the woods. Advise caution. The killer is armed with a longbow. Over."

I couldn't hear the other side of the conversation, but whatever they said, Campbell nodded.

"Contact the police, and have an ambulance dispatched," he said. "We have one fatality on site, over."

Alice and Rupert approached the body. Alice gasped when she saw Ben on the ground. "Did you see who shot Ben?"

"No. I think the arrows came from that direction." I pointed to the woods. "I saw two things fly out of the trees."

"There's only one arrow," Campbell said. "Princess Alice and Lord Rupert, you must stay with everyone else until backup has arrived. Everyone is vulnerable out here. The attacker may be looking for their next victim."

"Why would they want to shoot either of us?" Alice asked.

Campbell inclined his head at me. "Holly, stand in front of Princess Alice."

"Hold on, you can't use Holly as a human shield." Rupert grabbed my arm and pulled me to his side.

"Lord Rupert, you are—"

"No! That isn't acceptable." Rupert drew himself up to his full height, which was still shorter than Campbell, but impressive to watch. "Holly must be kept safe, too."

"Quite right," Alice said. "If anyone shoots at me, I'll shoot right back. And I'll hit them."

Campbell sighed. "At least stay together. You're more vulnerable on your own." He turned and scanned the trees again.

"Granny predicted this," Alice said. "She was right. I should have listened to her."

"So should I," I said. "Maybe I could have persuaded Ben not to take part in the contest."

"What are you talking about?" Campbell asked, his back still to us.

"Granny came over funny yesterday," Alice said. "She predicted Ben was going to die. Holly, you were there, tell Campbell what happened. I missed the start of her vision."

I resisted the urge to step back as Campbell glared at me. "It's true. I took Lady Philippa to the last evening lecture. She sat next to Ben. Everything was fine to begin with, but then she went pale and we had to leave. She said she knew Ben would die."

Campbell shook his head. "Unless Lady Philippa was the one who let loose the arrow that killed Ben, she can't have known this would happen."

"This is exactly what she predicted," Alice said.

"Lady Philippa even said Ben would die among the trees in the grounds of the castle," I said. I had no idea how Lady Philippa was able to predict these things, but a shudder ran down my spine. It was uncomfortably spooky how often she was right. I'd always considered myself a logical person, but maybe I needed to be more open-minded about this.

"We must account for everyone's whereabouts," Campbell said. "Who's missing from the party?"

I looked around the small group that remained. "Professor Stephen and his wife headed back to the castle a few minutes ago. Johann and Marcel are in the woods collecting arrows. Penny is somewhere taking a call, and Eddie is in the woods, too. That's everyone, isn't it?"

Rupert nodded. "That's right."

"Poor Penny," Alice said. "She'll be devastated when she comes back and sees Ben like this. They were so sweet together."

"Someone should find her. Tell her what's happened." I took a step toward the trees but stopped when Campbell lifted a hand and shook his head.

"We stay together until backup gets here," Campbell said. "If the shooter is still out there, my men will get him."

"Or her," Alice said. "What if Penny killed Ben?"

"Why would she do that?" I asked.

"I don't know. But as I've demonstrated, women can shoot just as well as men. And you need to be a good shot from a long distance. You have to account for drift and wind currents. Plus, you have the trees acting as natural barriers."

"You said she didn't know how to shoot a longbow," I said.

"I'm just saying, don't be too quick to discount the fairer sex," Alice said. "We can be lethal, too."

"Don't I know it," Campbell muttered. His gaze constantly scanned the surrounding trees.

I was doing the same, my panic making me paranoid, worried that more arrows would come shooting toward us.

"What's going on?" Johann emerged from the trees, closely followed by Marcel. "I saw one of the security chaps racing around in the woods. He told us to come back here immediately."

"Hey! Is that Ben on the ground?" Marcel asked. "What happened to him?"

Campbell strode over and brought them to the group. "There's been an incident. I need you both to stay here for now."

"An incident?" Marcel's mouth fell open and the color drained from his face. "That's an arrow sticking out of Ben's chest."

"Someone shot him," Alice said. "Where have both of you been hiding?"

Johann ran a hand down his face as he stared at Ben. "In the woods. I can't believe this. He's... dead?"

"Did either of you see anything?" I asked at the same time as Campbell.

Campbell glared at me and shook his head, his fierce gaze telling me to butt out.

"Oh! No, I didn't see anything," Johann said. "I mean, I didn't see anyone shooting at Ben. How... why did this happen?"

"The same here," Marcel said. "Shouldn't we cover him up? It doesn't seem right leaving the poor guy on the ground like that."

"What were you doing in the woods for so long?" Campbell asked.

"Collecting these." Marcel held up a dozen arrows.

"I took a while to find my lucky arrow," Johann said, his tight expression fixed on Ben. "This must have been an accident. Did Ben stray into the shooting range when he shouldn't have?"

"No," Alice said. "The arrow that killed him came from the trees behind the shooting range. Someone was aiming for him."

"Perhaps it was a rogue arrow." Johann tugged at his collar. "The wind can carry the arrows too far. It happens to me all the time."

I looked around the clearing. I was certain I'd seen two arrows, or at least, two fast moving blurs, seconds before Ben was struck. Maybe someone had tried to hit Ben and missed, so they'd had to shoot at him again.

"This must have been a misfire," Marcel said. His gaze went to Alice, who had picked up the longbow she'd given Ben to try.

"Don't look at me. I had nothing to do with this," she said. "I'm an excellent shot. Ten times better than both of you. Besides, I was here, standing with Rupert and Holly when Ben was hit. And I'm telling you, the arrow wasn't fired by any of us."

Meatball started barking, bouncing around and yapping at something on the ground not far from Ben's body.

"What's got into him?" Campbell said. "Keep him out of the way, or he'll disturb evidence."

I marched over and discovered Meatball tugging at something in the ground. "What have you got there?" I knelt and brushed aside a few dried leaves. There was an arrow lodged in the ground a few feet from where Ben had been standing just before he was shot.

Meatball grabbed the arrow shaft and tried to pull it out.

"No, you don't." I scooped him up and stepped back. "That's evidence."

"What have you got there?" Campbell walked over.

"I told you I saw two arrows. Meatball's just discovered the other one. The shooter failed to hit Ben the first time."

Campbell stared at the arrow before grunting. "Back away and take your dog with you. There could have been fingerprints on that arrow. The only thing we'll find now is dog drool."

"You should have listened to me and let me hunt for the second arrow, then any evidence would have been preserved."

Campbell opened his mouth but then nodded and turned away.

I cuddled Meatball as he squirmed and licked my cheek, seeming excited to discover such a crucial piece of evidence. "You're a good boy. Well done for finding the evidence that Campbell didn't believe existed."

"I didn't say that," Campbell said, his back still to me. "I was focused on making sure everyone was safe."

I was quiet for a moment as I watched him work, marking the evidence site before stepping back.

"Maybe I can help," I said. "I've already got a few ideas about who wanted Ben dead."

"Keep your ideas to yourself," he said. "My men will find the shooter and bring him or her back."

I lifted a shoulder before turning and walking back to Rupert and Alice. I wasn't surprised that Campbell was telling me to keep my nose out. He always did when I offered my help.

"What did you find?" Alice asked.

"A second arrow lodged in the ground," I said.

"Which means that whoever wanted Ben dead failed with their first shot," Rupert said.

"These longbows can make it tricky to be accurate when you're standing far away," Alice said. "Or maybe whoever fired the arrows, isn't a great shooter. Which means, I'm one hundred percent ruled out as a suspect."

"No one would think you could be involved in this," Rupert said. "Stop trying to draw attention to yourself."

"I'm not! I just want to make it clear that I'm innocent. After all, I'm the best longbow shooter here," Alice said, giving him a less than gentle shove.

The sound of footsteps crunching through leaves had me looking up.

Eddie emerged through the trees, balancing a dozen arrows in his arms. He stopped walking and looked around the group. "What's wrong? Why is everyone staring at me?"

Campbell strode toward him, and Eddie backed up. "Hold it right there."

"What?" Eddie continued to move backward. "I've not done anything wrong."

"Then you won't mind answering a few questions," Campbell said.

Eddie's gaze went to Ben, and his mouth fell open. He dropped the arrows, turned, and raced into the trees.

"Drayton, we've got a suspect on the run," Campbell said into his comms device. "He's heading in a south-easterly direction away from the castle. Focus on him."

Campbell remained in the clearing, his hands clenched. I could tell he longed to chase after Eddie but didn't want to leave us unprotected.

Alice grabbed my arm and leaned close. "Are you going to investigate this murder?"

"No! I don't want to get in Campbell's way on this one. He must be raging mad that this shooting happened on his watch."

"Don't you feel guilty?" Alice asked.

"What do I need to feel guilty about?" I turned and stared at her.

"Weren't you supposed to save Ben's life?"

"Alice! Of course I wasn't."

She twisted a curl around one finger. "I thought Granny asked you to look out for him."

My shoulders slumped, and I sighed. I did feel bad. "I didn't know this would happen. Even if I did know Ben was about to take an arrow in the chest, how could I have stopped it? Asked him to wear an arrow proof vest? Chained him to his bed so he couldn't take part today? I've tried to warn people when Lady Philippa has had predictions about them. It never ends well."

"None of this is your fault," Rupert said. "It's just terrible luck. Ben was in the wrong place at the wrong time."

"This was no accident," Alice said. "Two arrows fired at the same location. One is careless. Two shows intent."

I nodded. "You're right. If it had been a single arrow, then we could have considered it an accident. This was deliberate. Someone wanted Ben dead."

Rupert shook his head. "Even so, you couldn't have prevented this. And if you'd tried, you'd have been at risk. Neither of us want you getting hurt, do we, Alice?"

"Absolutely not," Alice said. "I'd much rather Ben was dead than you."

"Thanks, I think," I said. "I wish I'd been able to stop this, though. I can't help but feel bad about it."

"Although you weren't able to stop it," Alice said, a sly look crossing her face, "maybe you could make amends by solving the murder. That would make everything right."

"Stop making Holly feel guilty," Rupert said. "Maybe she doesn't want to deal with something so gruesome."

I tipped my head back, feeling a little conflicted. "It wouldn't do any harm to ask a few questions. It's the least I can do, find out what happened, and make sure Ben's killer gets what they deserve."

Alice clapped her hands together and bounced on her toes. "Absolutely. How exciting. Let's go hunt for a murderer."

Chapter 7

Meatball stirred me from my sleep by bouncing on the end of the bed and giving a quiet bark.

I rolled over and checked the time before groaning and pulling the covers over my head. "It's just gone five o'clock. You can't need to go outside just yet."

He barked again as he scurried up the bed, tugged the covers down, and licked my nose.

I petted his head to comfort him in the hope of getting at least another hour of sleep. As I ran my hand down his back, I noticed his hackles were raised. I opened one eye. "Is something wrong?"

He jumped off the bed and ran out the bedroom.

I rolled onto my back, my eyes just closing again, when a thump had me jerking upright.

Meatball barked from the lounge.

There was someone at my front door. I frowned as I sat up. Who was trying to get me out of bed at such a horribly early hour?

I yawned as I pulled on my dressing gown and shoved my feet into my slippers, before shuffling to the front door. I peered out the side window, and my eyes widened. Alice stood outside.

I unlocked the door and yanked it open. "Is everything okay?"

"Good morning to you, too," she said.

"You're never out of bed this early. I figured something must be up." I gestured for her to come into my apartment.

Meatball ran around her several times, his little tail wagging.

She walked in, a picnic basket nestled in the crook of one elbow, before giving him a pet. "I thought we could get a jump on the killer by having an early start."

I tipped my head back and groaned. "You're not getting the jump on any killer. Campbell can't find out we're doing this, and he definitely can't find out you're involved. He won't be happy if a member of the family he's supposed to protect is messing about in a murder investigation."

Alice set the picnic basket on the table and turned to me. "Campbell worries about nothing. Although it is sweet that he watches out for me. It shows he cares."

"It also shows he's doing the job he's paid to do." I ran my hands over my bed-messy hair. "What's in the basket?"

"Our breakfast. I snuck into the kitchen and convinced one of the staff to fill it with delicious treats. It's just what we need before we go on our adventure."

"Alice, hunting a killer isn't an adventure. It can be dangerous, as I've found out to my cost." I peered in the basket. My mouth watered at the croissants, cherry scones, and Danish pastries. Maybe I could forgive her for waking me so early.

"It's not my fault you get yourself in these sticky situations." She pointed at the kettle. "You make the tea, while I set the food out."

"Yes, your majesty." I did a mock curtsy before pulling out the tea things and brewing a strong pot of English breakfast tea.

"You have to admit, this is exciting," she said. Her smile faded when she spotted my stern look. "Of course, Ben's death was sad. We spoke during the shooting contest. He seemed nice. I can't imagine why anyone would want to kill him."

"I've got a few ideas." I took out plates and cutlery and set the table.

"I knew you'd be thinking about suspects." Alice settled in a seat. "Do you think Eddie had anything to do with it?"

I joined her and poured out the tea before making sure Meatball had plenty of food in his bowl so he wouldn't beg too much while we ate. "I heard from Betsy, who heard from a friend in the pub, that Drayton caught up with Eddie," I said. Betsy Malone, head cleaner at the castle, was a source of excellent gossip.

"Yes, I heard the same thing late last night." Alice passed me a croissant. "Campbell is very interested in Eddie as the killer. What do you think?"

"It was strange how he made a run for it," I said. "It doesn't suggest his innocence."

"I overheard security talking last night," Alice said. "Apparently, Eddie has a criminal past."

I swirled honey on my croissant. "Maybe he wasn't running because he'd killed Ben. He was worried the police would think the worst because of his record."

"He's not been charged with anything yet." Alice spoke around a mouthful of scone. "I overheard that as well."

I tilted my head as I replayed Ben's murder in my head. "I'm not sure it could have been Eddie who fired those arrows. It happened so fast, though, it was hard to get a fix on where they came from. I'd guess they were shot from behind the shooting range on the right-hand side. Eddie came out of the woods on the left of the targets."

"He could have moved after taking the shot. Longbow arrows are slower than recurve bow arrows when you release them," Alice said. "They travel slower because of their additional weight. It takes about a second for an arrow to reach a target that's one hundred meters away."

I shook my head and grinned at her. "Don't ever let anyone tell you you're just a pretty face."

"You think I'm pretty?"

I lifted my gaze to the ceiling. "Trust you to focus on that."

She giggled. "There was barely any wind yesterday. The conditions were perfect for an accurate shot if the shooter was experienced."

"And we have to assume they knew what they were doing and didn't just get lucky," I said. "Ben was standing to the right of the shooting range. The arrows came from his right. When Eddie appeared, he was on the far left of the shooting range."

"He could have come from that direction to make it look like he was innocent," Alice said. "Although that's quite a distance to run."

"And he wasn't out of breath when he came out of the woods," I said.

"And then there's the question of his motive," Alice said. "Why would Eddie kill Ben?"

"Because of Penny," I said. "Eddie hasn't hidden the fact he's interested in her."

"Oh, yes. You mentioned that," Alice said. "You think Eddie killed Ben because he wants Penny all to himself?"

I loaded up my croissant with more honey and took a bite. "It's not an amazing motive. I didn't get the impression he was all that serious about Penny. When I heard him talking to her, he was suggesting a no-strings kind of relationship. All the fun and tickle without any of the responsibility, if you get what I mean."

"I absolutely do," Alice said. "Men like that aren't to be trusted. They probably want to have some fun and tickle in every place they visit, leaving a string of broken hearts behind them. Penny was right to stay away from him."

"I could understand him wanting to harm Ben if he'd been pursuing Penny for a long time, but not for a brief fling."

"Eddie could have a temper. He didn't like being told no by Penny, so took his anger out on Ben."

"It's worth speaking to Eddie. Do you know if Campbell has taken Eddie to the police station?"

"They questioned him and let him go," Alice said. "He's most likely back at the castle dismantling the rest of the conference equipment."

"We should speak to him now," I said. "Before he leaves."

"There's no hurry," Alice said. "Half the equipment is still up in the library. Everything got put on hold after the murder. And we've got this food to eat first. And you need a shower."

I frowned at her. "I would have had a shower if someone hadn't woken me at the crack of dawn to discuss murder."

She finished her croissant and grabbed another one. "The early bird catches the killer. Besides, we need to get ahead of Campbell."

"You're always so eager to beat him," I said.

"So are you."

"Only because his smug alpha male ways rub me the wrong way. I like to show him he's not the only one who can solve a puzzle."

Alice dropped her gaze to her plate and her mouth twisted to the side. "Same here."

I recognized that look. "Alice, you can't seriously be in love with Campbell."

"No one's talking about love," she said. "But I do get a bit weak at the knees when he's all protective around me. I love it when he takes charge of a situation. It brings out the best in him."

"If you consider the best his grumpy, surly side and the fact he snaps at anyone if they get in his way," I said.

"He snaps because he cares," she said.

"Hmm, we're going to have to disagree on that." I selected an apricot Danish pastry that was bursting with plump raisins and glistened with a sweet glaze. It looked like one I'd made in the kitchen yesterday. "Why has everyone suddenly got the hots for Campbell, anyway?"

Alice's eyes widened. "Who else likes him? Don't say I have a rival."

I daren't mention Louise's name in front of Alice. She'd only just forgiven me for being friends with her. "As you said, some women find his behavior attractive. And he's a single guy, as far as I know. He's going to draw attention."

"It's his muscles. I like a man who looks after himself." She pursed her lips and jabbed her knife into a croissant. "Perhaps I should ask him out. Make things official. That would stop any rival in her tracks. No one would dare try to steal a princess's boyfriend."

My eyebrows rose slowly. "Will your family be happy about you dating a member of the security team?"

"Mommy and Daddy are away in Dubai for three months," Alice said. "They won't have a clue who I'm dating."

"But the Duke and Duchess are keeping an eye on things," I said. "They're your guardians. They have a responsibility to keep your parents informed."

"And they also have a responsibility to see me happy," she said. "Although I do need to be careful. With two unsuccessful engagements behind me, I don't want to look like the weird one in the family."

"It's too late for that. You're definitely the weird one," I said.

"I suppose I am. Especially since my best friend is a servant in the kitchen I'm the mistress of." She laughed and threw a grape at me.

"I'm always happy to serve," I said. "Let's finish this breakfast. I have a long overdue shower to take. Then we'll head to the castle and find Eddie."

"And interrogate him," Alice said.

"And ask him a few casual questions, while trying not to get noticed by your security."

"You're no fun."

"I'm lots of fun. I just don't have the protection of the household behind me if this all goes wrong."

"You have me. I'm protection enough." Alice tossed a piece of croissant for Meatball. "And you have Mr. Fluffball down there. He'll defend you with his little paws until the very end."

I could only nod in agreement as I ate more Danish pastry. I had an excellent support team behind me.

An hour later, we were all fed, and I was dressed and showered as we left my apartment. Meatball trotted along with us, happy to be out on an early walk.

Our timing was perfect. The work crew was just arriving to take down the rest of the staging equipment inside the castle. There was a group of six guys walking in ahead of us, most of them clutching coffee mugs and yawning.

"There's Eddie," Alice said. "Let's grab him before he starts work."

"How will we explain being in the library so early?" I asked.

"I live in this castle. I can go anywhere I like," Alice said. "It's perfectly within my rights to watch the work crew and make sure they don't damage any of the expensive wallcoverings or curtains. If anyone questions why I'm here, they're an idiot."

I grinned. "I'll let you tell them that."

We headed along the corridor and into the library. Eddie was at the end of the room by the temporary stage. He set his mug down and stared at the scaffolding in front of him.

"I'm so glad to see you here," Alice said as she strode over.

He glanced our way, then did a double-take. "You're that princess, aren't you? I've seen that big oil painting of you in the corridor. And you were at the shooting contest."

She did a little bob in front of him. "That's right. I'm Princess Alice Audley."

Eddie scrubbed the stubble on his chin. His gaze shifted to me. "I also recognize you. You and your dog were hassling me the other morning."

"Not hassling," I said. "Simply making sure there were no problems."

He did a half shrug. "Whatever. I need to get on with my work. This was supposed to be finished yesterday, but what with that mess in the woods, we got behind. The security here is insane for dragging me into that nightmare."

"They're perfectly sane. We make sure they undergo psychological assessments before they take up their duties in the castle," Alice said.

"Huh?" Eddie said.

"Why did you run when my security detail wanted to speak to you yesterday?" Alice asked.

I bit my bottom lip. Sometimes, Alice didn't know the meaning of subtlety.

Eddie huffed out a breath. "Official types like that enjoy pinning trouble on me. They get off on it. It's a power trip to them, trying to subdue the working class."

"Do they pick on you because of your tattoos?" Alice asked. "I see some on your arms and neck. Do you have them all over your body?"

He snorted a laugh. "They don't help. Do you want to take a look, Princess?" Eddie smirked at her.

"Oh! No, I don't want to see your tattoos. But maybe the police think they're gang marks. Don't gang members have tattoos on their body to show their affiliations?"

I glanced at her. I wasn't sure where she was getting her information from, but it made sense.

"I guess so. But these tattoos have nothing to do with being in a gang," Eddie said. "I just like getting ink. The police make assumptions, just like your security team did."

"You running off wasn't the best way to show you were innocent," I said.

"I soon figured that out," Eddie said. "The guy who caught up with me almost broke my arm as he held me down."

"You understand why he did it," Alice said. "Someone was killed."

"There's nothing to say it wasn't an accident," Eddie said. "Why think the worst?"

"Two arrows were fired at the victim," I said. "One could be considered a horrible piece of luck. Two was deliberate."

His eyebrows flashed up. "Someone targeted Ben? I hadn't heard about that. The guys who questioned me told me nothing. They took me to the station and asked all kinds of questions about my relationship with Ben and what problem I had with him. I kept telling them I didn't do it. I didn't even know the guy."

"But you know his girlfriend," I said. "I saw you talking to Penny."

He turned fully toward me and crossed his arms over his chest. "I didn't exactly know her, not in the way that could have been fun."

"Did Ben find out you were making moves on his girlfriend?" I said.

"What if he did? The guy was a geek. He couldn't have done anything to stop me if I wanted her."

"Penny was doing a good enough job of stopping you herself," I said. "And I expect when you talked to the police, they were interested in your connection to Penny. Or did you keep that from them?"

He grunted. "Why tell them? It meant nothing. I'm not gonna kill a guy to get to his girl. That's too much hard work. There are plenty more chicks to choose from."

"It is a motive for murder," I said. Not a great one, though, but I was willing to give Eddie a little shove and see if he had a temper.

"You're as bad as the security lurking around here, just waiting to point the finger and think the worst," Eddie said.

"Do you know how to shoot a longbow?" Alice asked.

Eddie tucked his hands into the back pockets of his jeans and rocked back on his heels. "What if I do?"

I hadn't expected that response. "You can really shoot one?"

His gaze narrowed, and he dropped his hands to his sides. "It's not only the posh lot who get to have fun with old weapons. I learned how to shoot when I was a kid. But I haven't held a bow in years."

"Where did you learn?" I asked.

He grinned. "Believe it or not, I was a boy scout. We did a week of outward bound stuff. I got good with a bow. The guy who ran the center was a history nut and had a load of replicas he let us use. It was fun. I don't shoot now."

"Maybe you prefer to use your fists than a bow." I nodded at Eddie's hands. "Where did you get those cuts and bruises?"

He lifted his hands and inspected them. "I do physical work. These come with the job."

He was lying. The swelling on his knuckles suggested he'd hit something with his fists. Could those bruises have been caused when he struck Ben? I'd noticed red marks on Ben's face shortly before he was killed.

Eddie glanced over our heads. "I need to get to work. My boss is watching."

I wasn't letting him go so easily. "Ben told you to keep away from Penny and you weren't happy about it. Did you have a word with him, and things got violent?"

Eddie shook his head. "I'm done with you two."

Meatball growled at Eddie, his hackles raising.

I rested a hand on Meatball's head to calm him.

"If you don't answer Holly, I can always check with my security team," Alice said. "They're obliged to tell me everything, especially if it pertains to my safety. They won't like it if they learn you were being difficult."

"If you don't think I'm safe to be around, you need to leave, Princess," Eddie said. "You came to hassle me. The guys in here will confirm my story if things get tricky."

"You didn't damage your hands fighting with Ben?" I asked.

Eddie scraped a hand over his cropped hair. "Fine. I guess it'll come out, anyway. Ben did talk to me. He told me to back off from Penny. I didn't like the tone in his voice, so I made sure he knew it."

"You fought Ben before he died?" Alice said.

"Yeah, and the idiot snitched on me to the police," Eddie said. "My foreman was furious. He threatened to fire me. If I wasn't so good at my job, he would have done."

"That's why the police and castle security are so interested in you," I said. "Did they know about the fight?"

"Of course they did," he said. "They kept asking me about it. But I didn't kill Ben. He told me to stay away from his girl, and I didn't like it. I taught him a lesson in good manners, but that was it. He got a few bruises and learned not to mess with me. But I draw the line at ending another guy's life. No woman is worth that."

"You were in the woods for a long time during the shooting competition," I said. "It can't take that long to find a few arrows."

He sighed. "It does the way those idiots were shooting."

"I'm an excellent shot," Alice said. "I never miss my target."

"Then maybe the cops should be grilling you," Eddie said. "You could have killed Ben."

"Alice was with me," I said.

He shrugged again. "Whatever. You did okay with your bow, but most of the others were lousy. And it's overgrown behind the shooting range. It took me a while to find everyone's arrows."

"Did anyone see you collecting the arrows at the time of the shooting?" I asked.

A sly smile crossed his face. "You should ask Penny. She wandered into the woods on her phone when I was searching for them. I couldn't miss that opportunity. I gave it one more try with her. I was chatting her up when her boyfriend was killed. How's that for an alibi?"

I glanced at Alice and raised my eyebrows. That would be easy to check. And although Eddie had been initially evasive, he was open enough about the fact he didn't like Ben and they'd fought.

"I have to get to work," Eddie said, a hint of desperation in his voice. "My boss has me on my final warning. This job isn't much, but it's all I've got."

"Is there anything else you wanted to ask, Holly?" Alice asked.

"No, that's all for now," I said.

His gaze ran over us. "What are you, some kind of Cagney and Lacey wannabes?"

"We're more like Turner and Hooch," I said. "She's Hooch."

Confusion crossed Alice's face. "Is that good?"

I hid a smile and nodded goodbye to Eddie. "It's excellent. Come on, let's get out of here." We turned and left the room.

"What do you think of him?" Alice asked.

"He's on the suspect list, especially if his alibi doesn't check out."

"I agree. Eddie has shady running through him. What's our next move?"

"I need to get to work," I said. "Unlike you, I don't own a castle and get to mooch around all day. If I turn up late, I don't get paid, and Chef Heston yells at me."

Alice swatted me with the back of her hand. "I never mooch. And I have singing practice in two hours. Maybe I could pretend I have a sore throat. Or we could swap places. I'd much rather be surrounded by yummy cake all day than endure the acid comments from Madame Damore when I hit the wrong note."

"Although I love to sing, your teacher won't be impressed with my out of tune wailing."

"We have to stay focused on this murder, though. We've made progress talking to Eddie."

"We need to find a way to speak to Penny," I said. "So we can check Eddie's alibi. If they were together when Ben was killed, it'll rule them both out as suspects."

"You focus on baking the delicious treats in the kitchen, I'll figure out how to get to Penny." Alice gave me a brief hug before hurrying away.

I shook my head as she skipped along the corridor. Only Alice could be so excited about murder. "Come on, Meatball. There's a rawhide chew with your name on it, and I need to get to the kitchen before we're late."

Chapter 8

"If I have to remind you one more time to keep an eye on those cakes in the oven, I'll dock your wages for insubordination." Chef Heston loomed over me.

I pulled myself upright and glanced at the oven. "I haven't forgotten about them. They need another five minutes."

"Which you'd have let drift past while you stared out the window. What's the matter with you? You've been like this ever since you arrived this morning."

He'd caught me red-handed neglecting my duties. My thoughts had been on Ben's murder. So far, I'd nearly burned two trays of cakes because I'd been distracted thinking about who killed him.

"Nothing, Chef. I'm focused on my work."

"Then act like you are. No more daydreaming." He glared at me before striding away.

I pushed Ben's murder to the back of my mind. I had several more hours before I could finish work, and I had half a dozen things still to tick off my to-do list.

The kitchen door opened, and Evelyn poked her head around it. "Is it okay if I come in? I got a bit lost. The castle is so big."

I hurried over and opened the door wider. "Of course. Is there something you need?"

"Actually, I'm looking for something to help my husband."

"Is his back still troubling him?" I asked.

"Oh, of course. I thought I recognized you." She smiled at me. "You were there yesterday at the shooting contest. You arrived with those delicious cakes."

"That's right. I'm Holly. This is my day job. I saw when Professor Stephen hurt his back."

"He's still in a bad way, but I'm more worried about his stress levels than his back. Given what happened to Ben, he barely slept last night. Neither of us did."

"Take a seat," I said. "Maybe some herbal tea will help him. Chamomile is good for stress."

"Thank you. That's kind of you. Chamomile will be perfect." She settled in a seat at the table and looked around at the activity in the kitchen. "You must be busy in here. I visited your café the first day I got here. It's very popular. I had to wait to get a seat."

"Sometimes, we can barely keep up with the orders," I said as I boiled the kettle. "We get visitors coming to the castle all year round."

"I can see why," Evelyn said. "It's such a beautiful place. You're lucky to live here."

I smiled as I placed loose leaf chamomile tea in a teapot and poured hot water on it. "I couldn't agree more. I sometimes have to pinch myself. Would you like a cup of this tea, too? I imagine your nerves are also frayed after what happened."

"I wouldn't say no," Evelyn said. "This whole situation is very trying."

I passed her a cup and sat opposite her. "Did you know Ben?"

"Not very well, but our paths crossed from time to time. He was a sweet young man. Very dedicated to his work. He would sometimes help out at the fundraising events I arrange."

"What do you fundraise for?"

"My husband's research," she said. "The grant funding isn't what it used to be, and Stephen has great ambitions. I hold two or three events each year to bring in high donors. They make donations to fund his projects. I enjoy it; it's like hosting a big party, but everyone presents you with money at the end of it. Ben helped out at the events when he had the time."

"That sounds like fun," I said. "I know a lot about Professor Stephen's work. I saw your husband give several lectures when I was at university."

"Oh! How lovely for you. Do you still have an interest in history?" She took a sip of her chamomile tea.

"I do. I didn't follow it as a career path, but being surrounded by history in the castle more than makes up for it."

"I was never one for a glittering career," Evelyn said. "I'm happy to support Stephen, but I'm not career driven. I like the simple things in life."

"I'm with you there. I also prefer a behind-the-scenes role, which is why I love being in the kitchen." I smiled at her, and she returned it warmly. "I've read all of your husband's books. I'm always impressed how he comes up with those new theories."

Evelyn leaned across the table before glancing around. "Don't tell anyone I said this, but I've never finished any of his books. I'm sure what he writes is brilliant, but I'm just not smart enough to understand it. I think he married me for my looks, not my intellect."

I grinned. "I'm sure that's not true."

"I know he loves me in his own way, but his career will always be his one true love."

"And you don't mind that?"

"Of course not. I'm happy if he's happy. But the poor lamb is definitely not happy at the moment. He's injured, and he's lost his best research student. He always praised Ben for his hard work. In fact, he never had a bad word to say about him. Ben's a real loss to the historical research community."

I sipped my tea. Evelyn seemed friendly. I should risk a few gentle questions while she was here.

"Did you see anyone acting suspiciously when you were in the woods? Anyone lurking around that made you worried?"

"You mean someone with a bow and arrow who was hunting Ben?"

I nodded. "Any clue could be helpful in finding out how this happened."

"I didn't see anything," she said. "Stephen was in a lot of discomfort, and I was focused on keeping him moving so we could get back to the castle and he could rest. We didn't know anything about what had happened to Ben until later. Stephen had been in bed for half an hour and was dozing off, when a member of the castle security team informed us."

That gave both of them an alibi for when Ben was killed. And given Professor Stephen's injury, there'd be no way he could fire a bow without causing himself a great amount of pain.

"Do you know of anyone who had a problem with Ben?" I asked.

Her forehead wrinkled, and she pursed her lips. "No one springs to mind. I did hear that the police were interested in one of the stage hands. He was helping at the shooting competition."

"Eddie. But I don't think they're pursuing that line of inquiry, anymore."

"So, the killer could still be out there?" Her gaze went to the window.

"It's possible. I wondered if Ben had any enemies, or someone who may have decided to target him at the contest."

"Goodness, you have given this some thought," Evelyn said.

"I can't stop thinking about it."

"I suppose I can't, either. To be honest, it's not sunk in yet. I still expect Ben to come bounding through a door, full of energy." She drank more tea. "There is always rivalry in academic circles over classifications, dates, and finds, but they fight it out in a civilized way, usually over a glass of wine. They don't go around shooting each other with arrows."

"That does sound civilized."

"And I can't think of anyone who had a problem with Ben. He was an affable young man. Always polite and pleasant. I feel so sorry for his girlfriend."

"I haven't seen Penny since it happened. Do you know how she's doing?"

"Neither have I," Evelyn said. "I believe she's still in her room. She's taken the news hard, understandably so."

"They weren't having relationship struggles?"

Evelyn's eyes widened. "No! They were adorable. Love's young dream. I just hope this turns out to be a terrible accident. It doesn't do to think that Ben was murdered."

It was a nice thought, if a bit naïve, given the evidence. "Let me get you a tray for the tea. Would you like any cake to go with it?"

"I wouldn't say no," Evelyn said. "Do you have any of that almond cake you served yesterday? That was tasty."

"Of course." I plated up four small cakes and set everything on a tray.

"Thanks. I appreciate you taking the time with me. I can see how busy you are."

"You're welcome," I said. "I hope Professor Stephen feels better soon."

"We were hoping to leave tomorrow, but he still can't walk far, so we may be stuck here for a couple more days. Not that you'll hear me complaining. Being stuck in a beautiful place like Audley St. Mary is hardly a chore." Evelyn stood and took the tray. "Thanks again for the tea." She smiled at me before leaving the kitchen.

I walked back to the table and drummed my fingers on the top. If Eddie and Penny alibied for each other, and Professor Stephen and Evelyn were together when Ben was killed, that wiped out nearly everyone involved in the shooting competition.

My gaze went to the oven. My heart lurched to the floor and ricocheted back into my chest. I hadn't been paying attention. The cakes were burning.

I checked Chef Heston wasn't around before grabbing an oven mitt, yanking open the oven door, and pulling out the tray. I grimaced as I set the cakes on the table. There'd be no way I could serve these overdone offerings to the tourists in the café.

I grabbed a bag, slid the overcooked cakes into it, and tucked it out of sight in my locker. The cakes may not be suitable for human consumption, but I knew a flock of doves who were regular visitors to the castle grounds. They'd appreciate them. Meatball probably wouldn't say no to a burned cake, either.

I dashed around, put together a new batch of cherry and caramel cake mixture, and placed the tray back in the oven. With luck on my side, Chef Heston wouldn't even notice.

My phone buzzed in my pocket, and I took it out.

Emergency situation. Need you in my room ASAP. Love Alice.

What had she gotten herself into? I texted back. *Be there in fifteen minutes. Currently on cake watch.*

Hurry! And bring cake.

Once the cakes were baked and set out on a cooling tray, I walked over to Chef Heston. "Is it okay if I take my fifteen-minute break now?"

He didn't even glance up from the vanilla sponge he was icing. "Is everything out of the oven?"

"All done. The cakes need time to cool before I decorate them."

"Fine. Take your break."

I took off my apron, hurried out of the kitchen and up to Alice's room with a plate of cherry cream tarts in my hand. I knocked on her door, opening it when she told me to.

Alice stood in the middle of the room. She flung her arms out wide. "Surprise!"

"Surprise? You said there was an emergency. Did you learn something about Ben's murder?" I shut the door behind me and hurried over.

Alice waved away my comments. "This emergency situation isn't about Ben. It's about you." She stepped to one side and gestured at two round stools with chunky legs that stood behind her.

"What are they?" The chairs had padded arms and sat low to the floor.

"A gift from me to you. Well, one of them is yours. I thought it would be fun if we had a chair each."

"I, um, thanks. I guess everyone can do with an extra chair. They're an unusual design."

"Take a seat. These are no ordinary chairs." Alice giggled as she settled on her own seat.

I set down the tarts and perched on the stool. "Are they massaging chairs? They seem a bit low to be comfortable to sit on for long."

"Nope, they don't massage. Now, hold on tight." Alice leaned over. "I'm not sure how fast these things go."

"Wait! What do you mean?" I grabbed the arms of my stool as it rotated in a fast circle.

Alice squealed as her chair whirred and spun. "What do you think?"

I let go of the arms and made sure I was balanced. "It's twirling me in a circle."

"That's exactly what it's supposed to do," she said. "It's a hula chair. You sit on it, and it does the hard work for you. It's a great way to tone your abs and core. I saw an ad for the chair and knew it would be perfect for you. You love trying new fitness things."

"A hula chair! I've never heard of such a thing. Where did you find it?" The chair shook me so hard my teeth rattled.

"I was up late watching a home shopping channel. They sell all kinds of bizarre things on there. Anyway, this woman came on and demonstrated these chairs. I was on the phone in seconds, ordering us two. I couldn't think of a more perfect gift. You get fit by sitting down."

All I was feeling was queasy as the chair shifted me from side to side. "Do they really work?"

"We'll find out in a few weeks. I'd love to get rid of my lower belly." Alice's gaze went to the plate I'd placed on her bed. "Pass me one of those tarts. I'm famished."

I laughed and shook my head before handing her a cherry cream tart. "Thanks for my chair. I love it. And since I'm here, I've got an update about Ben."

"Tell me everything." Alice bit into the tart, almost missing her mouth when her chair groaned and spun faster.

"Evelyn came into the kitchen a little while ago, and we had a chat. She seems nice."

"Yes, I like her, too," Alice said. "She was fun to spend time with at the shooting contest."

"I managed to get an alibi for Evelyn and Professor Stephen. They were together when Ben was killed. They didn't know what happened until they got back to the castle."

"So we can rule them out as having anything to do with his murder?" Alice said.

"I think so."

"I'm not surprised. I don't think Evelyn shoots, anyway. Professor Stephen definitely does, but he's not very good. He'd have needed luck on his side to hit Ben."

"And he's also injured," I said.

Alice finished her tart and hopped off the hula seat. "Hold on to your murderous thoughts for a moment. I got you something else."

I tried to turn in my seat and almost fell off. I grabbed hold of the arms. "What else have you got me?"

She opened her large closet and pulled out a beautiful shimmering pink mermaid tail. "What do you think of this?"

"Alice! That's stunning. You really got that for me?"

She nodded, walked over, and held it out in front of me. "I would never have known about mermaid school if it weren't for you. And I did say I'd get us tails. I found a woman who specializes in making them. I got one for myself in purple and blue. We'll have to try them out in the lake when it's warmer."

I stroked my hand along the soft glistening scales. It looked handcrafted and was nothing like the cheap tails I'd been researching online. "It must have been expensive. I love it. Alice, this is too much. You shouldn't have gotten me something so extravagant."

"Yes, I should. The hula chair and the mermaid tail are my way of making it up to you. I was a bad friend, and that was wrong of me. I don't want you not to like me anymore."

I hopped off the vibrating stool and hugged her. "I'll always like you. You don't have to buy me things to keep my friendship."

She hugged me back. "I want to get you presents. Besides, I like buying things. And I also got myself a tail and a hula chair, so it wasn't purely selfless. I can hardly be a mermaid on my own, can I?"

I kissed her cheek, then stood back to admire my beautiful tail some more. "I absolutely adore it. Thank you."

"Excellent." Alice placed the tail back in the closet. "I'll keep them both in here until we find time to go swimming. Now, back to the murder. I've been working on something that'll help us solve this mystery."

My eyes narrowed. "What have you been up to?"

She grinned and bounced on her toes. "Everything is lined up. All you need to do is turn up and speak to the suspect."

I always got nervous when Alice made plans. "Turn up where? And talk to whom?"

She clapped her hands together. "I've invited Penny for afternoon tea, and you're going to serve it to us."

Chapter 9

An hour after my conversation with Alice, I wheeled a trolley loaded with afternoon tea delicacies out of the kitchen.

I had to admit, her scheme to get Penny alone was clever. And I didn't mind playing the role of server. It meant I got to listen into the conversation. I'd be able to see if Penny was hiding any secrets that gave us a clue about what had happened to Ben.

I knocked at the Little Drawing Room door and waited until Alice announced I could enter.

The room had a recess at the back, which contained a lavishly embroidered couch, which looked out onto the manicured gardens. The ceiling and walls were decorated with Roman motifs designed from Italian originals, and the furnishing matched the gold frames of the wall panels.

Alice and Penny sat at a small gold-legged table by the large window.

"Excellent. The tea is here. I've been looking forward to this all day," Alice said.

"I don't have much of an appetite," Penny said, dark circles marring her petite features.

"I'm sure these treats will tempt you," Alice said. "It's good not to be alone at a difficult time like this. This is just what you need. You may serve us, Holly."

I wheeled the trolley in and stopped by the table.

Penny chewed on her bottom lip before nodding. "You're right. I was so stunned after what happened to Ben that I hid away. That only made me feel worse."

"You shouldn't be on your own." Alice reached over and patted her hand. "When my first engagement failed, I stayed in bed for a week feeling sorry for myself and eating chocolate."

"Oh! I didn't know you were engaged," Penny said. "I follow the society news and never saw an announcement."

"Would you both like tea?" I set out the cups and plates and held aloft the teapot, giving Alice a pointed look. She was supposed to be talking about Ben, not her own checkered love life.

"Yes, please." Alice smiled brightly. "I've actually been engaged twice. Both were spectacular failures."

Penny sighed. "I imagine neither of your fiancés died?"

"Oh! No, nothing like that," Alice said. "It was still a gruesome time. A sad time, and it did me no good to hide away from people."

I repressed a smile and poured the tea. Alice never did well when it came to romantic relationships. She tried hard to find the men her parents chose for her suitable, but while she was lusting after Campbell, there wasn't much hope for anyone else.

Alice lifted her cup. "My first fiancé owns most of the land down in Hampshire."

"He must be terribly rich." Penny helped herself to a cherry scone from the plate I set down.

"Almost as rich as me," Alice said. "The problem was, he was more interested in his working dogs than having a relationship with me. And he had a lisp. I tried to get past those things and see his good points, but it was never going to work between us."

I discreetly cleared my throat.

Alice ignored me. "And then there was my second engagement, which I should never have agreed to. He had a weak chin, a pot belly, and a receding hairline. My parents selected him because of his connections. I kept telling them I planned to marry for love, but they wouldn't listen to me. In the end, they wore me down, and I agreed to the engagement. Neither of us were happy, and after a few disastrous dates, we realized it wouldn't work. I called it off and then got accused of being a flip-flop by my family. It was heart-breaking."

"You deserve to be happy," Penny said. "You shouldn't marry someone you don't love."

"I agree. But I've still not found a man I want to marry." Alice's eyes sparkled. "Although there is someone I'm interested in. His name—"

"Would you like a cherry scone, Princess Alice?" I thrust the plate at her before she blundered on and revealed her crush on Campbell.

"Oh! Yes, thank you." She took a scone, ate a piece, and frowned, before setting it to one side.

"Is there anything else I can do for you, Princess Alice?" I couldn't tell her point blank to start questioning Penny, but I'd have to do something drastic if she didn't get a move on.

She glanced up at me, and her eyes widened. "Yes! Cut up my scone. And it's a little dry. Put plenty of clotted cream on it. Otherwise, I won't be able to eat it."

"Of course." I set to work on her scone.

Alice took a sip of her tea and shifted in her seat. "Penny, tell me all about Ben. It'll do you good to talk about him. How long were you seeing each other?"

Penny let out a long sigh. "Two years. We met at university. I'd only just started my history PhD and had been there a week when I met him."

"Was it love at first sight?" Alice asked.

Penny ducked her head. "It was for me. It took Ben a little time to warm up. He was devoted to his research. That was one of the many things I liked about him. He had such a passion for his work."

"That didn't get in the way of your relationship?" Alice said.

I smiled and nodded. At last, we were making progress.

"It did at times, but I only wanted the best for Ben," Penny said. "He was always worrying about his research, though. More so recently. I thought it was the stress of handling the history conference that was getting to him. There were so many people to manage, and Ben was never great in crowds. He was an introvert. Big groups of people exhausted him."

I handed Alice the plate with the scone on. "Is that suitable, Princess Alice?"

"Perfect, thank you," Alice said. "I noticed the napkins on your trolley aren't folded correctly. Deal with those before you leave."

I bobbed my head. "Of course."

Alice smiled at Penny. "Was anything else worrying Ben?"

Penny glanced at me before continuing. "Ben wasn't sleeping well. He also seemed jumpy. It was as if he expected something bad to happen."

"Do you think someone threatened him?" Alice leaned forward in her seat. "Could he have been concerned for his safety?"

The trace of color in Penny's cheeks vanished. "He didn't mention anything like that to me. I suppose it's possible. But why?"

"Could it have been Eddie?" Alice asked. "Castle security is interested in him. And he's a criminal. I also know he's been a problem for you," Alice said.

Penny blinked away tears. "Eddie was a big problem for me, but not only me. Ben didn't want me to know, but Eddie bullied him. He was trying to chase him away."

"So he could get to you?" Alice asked.

"I believe so," Penny said on a sigh. "I wasn't interested in Eddie, but the man couldn't take a hint."

"I understand Eddie roughed Ben up when he told him to stay away from you," Alice said.

Penny was quiet for several seconds. "True. You are well-informed."

"This is my home. It's important I know what's going on."

Penny shook her head. "I wish he hadn't gone after Eddie. I didn't ask him to. Ben wasn't a fighter, but he said he had to defend my honor."

"That's very sweet," Alice said. "I like a man who'll look after me if ever I need him to."

"I suppose it was," Penny said, "but I know Eddie's type. He uses his fists and threats to get what he wants. Ben was out of his depth, and Eddie was quick to show him that."

"My security told me that Eddie used you as his alibi for Ben's murder," Alice said. "Is that true?"

She sucked in a breath, grabbed a napkin, and dabbed at her overflowing eyes. "I did see him in the woods just before Ben was shot. I took a call from my best friend. She's been having trouble in her relationship and needed a shoulder to cry on. I walked into the woods so I could hear her properly. I saw Eddie, and he was quick to come over and try to sweet talk me. I was still on the phone, so didn't pay him much attention."

"Was he acting suspiciously?" Alice asked.

"Not that I could see," Penny said. "But I wasn't with him for long. He walked over, hung around for a moment, and then wandered off when I ignored him."

"Did he have a longbow with him?" Alice asked.

I raised my eyebrows and nodded again. Alice was getting the hang of this interviewing business.

"Oh! No, not that I saw. But he had plenty of arrows. It wouldn't have been hard to conceal a bow in the overgrown bushes at the back of the shooting range," Penny said.

"I hope you don't think me impertinent, but Eddie is attractive," Alice said. "Are you sure you weren't a tiny bit tempted by someone so hot and dangerous? After all, we all love a bad boy."

Penny jerked back in her seat and frowned. "I have zero interest in Eddie. Ben was the only one for me. He may not have been tall or muscular, but he was my soulmate. We'd planned to spend the rest of our lives together." Her chin dropped to her chest. "Now, I'm not sure what I'll do without him."

Alice glanced at me, concern in her eyes.

Penny had an alibi, and it would be easy for Campbell or the police to check her phone records and see who she was talking to. And the fact she'd seen Eddie in that part of the woods also made it unlikely he was the killer. Plus, he'd had no weapon on him.

"Let's have more cake," Alice said. "I always feel better once I've had cake."

Penny dabbed at her nose with the napkin. "I do feel better talking to you. Thank you for inviting me this afternoon. It's very thoughtful of you."

"You're most welcome," Alice said. "Holly, please cut the crusts off this sandwich. You know I don't like the crusts."

"Of course, Princess Alice." I was glad she'd given me a job to do. I was running out of reasons to hang around and listen to the conversation.

Penny looked at me and then back at Alice. "You get your staff to do a lot for you."

"Holly enjoys it," Alice said. "She likes to be kept busy."

"I'm always happy to serve," I said as meekly as I could. I handed the crustless sandwich back to Alice.

A movement at the window caught my eye. I turned and swallowed down a gasp. Campbell stood outside. And from the look on his face, he wasn't happy to see what Alice and I were up to.

"What sort of research was Ben doing?" Alice asked, oblivious to the angry glares shooting into the room. "His work couldn't have been what got him in trouble, could it?"

"I don't think his studies had anything to do with his death," Penny said. "Ben was producing a new paper and possibly a book from his latest research. He was very excited. He'd applied for a large grant to help finalize his project. He had such a bright future. Not anymore." A small sob escaped her lips.

"You could carry on his work for him," Alice said. "It would be a nice way to remember Ben."

"I'm not half as clever as Ben was. I wouldn't be able to do his work justice." She sniffed and lifted her head. "Eddie has to be involved with this. I can't think of anyone else who would want Ben dead."

"I'm sure we'll find out what happened soon enough," Alice said. "The castle security team is excellent. We only hire the best, and they work alongside the local police to make sure things happen quickly. We'll find out who did this."

"I really hope you do. Ben deserved better than this. He was a nice guy, and this shouldn't have happened to him." She stood and pushed her seat back. "If you'll excuse me. I need some time on my own."

"Of course." Alice accompanied Penny to the door. "Any time you want to chat, I'm here. And stay in the castle for as long as you like. I don't want you to leave before you're ready."

"Thanks. That's good of you," Penny said. "I have to sort out Ben's things before I leave. I'll be here a few more days."

"Take as long as you need." Alice said goodbye to Penny before closing the door behind her.

"So, what do you think?" I asked.

Alice returned to her seat, her lips pursed. "I think that you definitely didn't make these scones. What were you doing, bringing someone else's scones to my afternoon tea party?"

I groaned. "Not about the food. What do you think about Penny and her alibi?"

Alice prodded the half-eaten scone on her plate before shoving it away. "Oh, well, she seems nice. And she's definitely sad about Ben being dead." She gestured at the seat Penny had vacated, and I sat in it.

"There's a motive here, though," I said. "Penny was open about Ben being obsessed with his work. Could she have been jealous that he loved the past more than their future together?"

"Oh! I hadn't picked up on that," Alice said. "I don't think it was Penny who fired that shot, though. She didn't take part in the shooting contest. I remember her saying she didn't know how to shoot a longbow. I even offered to show her how to do it, so I could get more girl power involved, but she said she was happy to observe. And you don't simply pick up a bow and fire a perfect shot the first time. It's impossible."

"Penny could be hiding her skills," I said. "And jealousy is a powerful motivator for murder."

"I'm still not buying it," Alice said. "Penny loved Ben. She could see a long and happy future with him. Why kill him because he got a bit obsessed with his research? A lot of men do that with their jobs."

"And a lot of wives divorce them, or have murderous thoughts about them because of it," I said. "A few even act on those thoughts."

"Penny pointed the finger firmly at Eddie," Alice said. "She doesn't like him."

"You can hardly blame Penny for that after he harassed her and beat up Ben," I said. "Although Eddie's alibi isn't watertight. Penny was on the phone, so that can be checked out, but since Eddie wandered off while she was talking to her friend, he could have fired the arrow that killed Ben."

"Eddie would have needed to be fast on his feet, though," Alice said. "And accurate with a bow. I suppose we can't rule either of them out just yet. But Penny doesn't seem the type. She's too sweet, and very unhappy about losing her boyfriend."

"Eddie's definitely not sweet, but neither Penny nor Eddie seem like likely suspects," I said. "We should move them to the bottom of the list for now."

"Agreed. But let's not scrub them off. Not until we know Penny's phone call was genuine."

"I'm sure Campbell and his team will be on that," I said.

There was a knock at the door.

"Come in," Alice said.

Campbell appeared in the doorway, his expression neutral, although I detected a glint of anger in his eyes.

"Sorry for the interruption. May I have a word with you, Miss Holmes?"

"Of course you may," Alice said. "She's right here. Have as many words as you like."

"In private, if you don't mind, Princess Alice," Campbell said.

I gulped and jumped to my feet. "I can't be long. I'm very busy in the kitchen."

"So it would appear," Campbell said. "I won't keep you. If you'll excuse us, Princess Alice."

She glanced up at me and shrugged. "Fine by me. I've got all this lovely cake to eat, although I'm not touching those rock-hard scones. I'll catch up with you later, Holly."

I nodded and followed Campbell out of the room. I had a feeling I was in big trouble.

Chapter 10

"Where are we going?" I hurried after Campbell as he marched out the main doors of the castle and along the gravel driveway, the small stones crunching under his feet.

"To the crime scene." He didn't look over his shoulder, his arms swinging by his side as he hurried along.

"Why are you taking me there?" Panic welled in my throat. I'd been an annoyance in Campbell's life ever since I'd started work at the castle. He had the means and the skills to shoot me and conceal the evidence. No one would ever find my body if Campbell decided to hide it. Well, maybe Meatball would. He'd be able to find me anywhere.

I took a steadying breath, slowing my jackhammer heart. Campbell could be mean, but he didn't have murderous intentions toward me. I had to hope that was true.

"It seems you can't keep out of this investigation, yet again," he said.

"I've kept right out of your way," I said. "I've barely spoken to you since Ben was shot."

"Very true. Instead, you've been speaking to the suspects," he said. "I just witnessed you talking to Penny."

"That had nothing to do with me," I said. "Princess Alice invited her to afternoon tea so she could check how she was doing. After all, Penny has just lost her boyfriend in tragic circumstances."

"Of course, that was all you were doing," he said. "Why were you serving the afternoon tea? You usually bake."

"Princess Alice insisted on it," I said. I was so dropping her in it, but Alice could get away with just about anything. "And you don't say no to her, or she threatens to send you to the dungeon."

He was silent for several seconds. "Did Penny tell you anything interesting that could aid the investigation?"

"If you slow down a bit, I might tell you." I was gasping for breath as we entered the woods and headed along the path toward the shooting range.

"You said you were busy." Campbell sped up. "I figured we needed to do this quickly."

He was such a show off. He wasn't even out of breath, and I was almost jogging to keep up with him and had a burning stitch in my side.

"So, what did Penny tell you?" he asked again.

"Why don't you tell me what she told you first?" I said. "I bet you've already interviewed her."

He slowed as we entered the clearing where the shooting range was set up. "She checks out fine. Penny was speaking to a friend on the phone at the time of the murder. We've checked her phone records. I don't consider her a suspect."

"What about the jealousy motive?" I leaned over and caught my breath as Campbell strode around, his gaze fixed on the trees.

He turned and arched an eyebrow before crossing his arms over his chest. "Keep talking."

I sucked in a deep breath and straightened. "Penny clearly loved Ben. She had big plans for their future.

Maybe she didn't like the fact his work came first. Everyone I've spoken to about Ben told me he was going places. Maybe he put their relationship on the back burner to focus on his career. Penny may not have liked that."

He shook his head. "She alibis out. And Eddie confirmed he saw her talking on the phone. She may not have liked Ben being a workaholic, but she's not the killer."

I nodded slowly. "I think you're right, but I wanted to cover all bases."

"I'm glad we can agree on something," he said.

I snorted a laugh. "Miracles do happen. So, why have you brought me out here?"

"To show you around the crime scene."

I took a step back. "Are you kidding me?"

"I don't kid. Let's move. We're both busy people."

I was so shocked that I didn't say anything as I stumbled along beside Campbell. He never let me in on the investigation side of things, not without much arm twisting and a few sneaky moves on my part.

"Let's set the scene." He stopped in the middle of the clearing. "Penny and Eddie were to the left of the shooting range. Eddie was collecting misfired arrows, and Penny was taking a call from a friend."

"That's right," I said.

"You were here with Princess Alice and Lord Rupert. Ben was to your right, messing around with Princess Alice's longbow."

"Right again," I said. "And you and Drayton were behind us, watching everything going on."

"Correct," he said.

"Then we had Marcel and Johann, who'd gone into the woods to find Johann's lucky arrow."

"Do you recall their location?" Campbell asked.

I scratched my head. All the moving parts were getting confusing. "Hold on a second." I grabbed a handful of stones, swiped my foot along the ground to make a clear patch, and kneeled. "These two stones represent Penny and Eddie." I placed them on the ground. "These three stones are me, Princess Alice, and Lord Rupert. The stones I'm putting behind us are you and Drayton."

"I'm with you so far," he said, a smirk on his face.

"Ben is this stone. He was the only one standing on his own. Then we have Marcel and Johann. They headed off in a similar direction to Professor Stephen and his wife."

"Who were taking a shortcut back to the castle because he'd hurt his back," Campbell said. He grabbed two stones from my hand and placed them to the right of the shooting range.

"We have to assume that Marcel and Johann were about here." I also placed two stones to the right of the shooting range. "That's everyone, isn't it?"

"Unless we have a mystery shooter who slipped in, fired the arrow that killed Ben, and then vanished, that's everyone accounted for," Campbell said.

"Wait! There's one more." I picked up a small stone and placed it near the trees. "Meatball."

Campbell scoffed. "He's a crucial piece of the puzzle."

"He did find the second arrow."

"You mean, he chewed on vital evidence and potentially ruined a crime scene."

"Meatball is a wonder dog, but he has his limits. He doesn't always know what's a clue and what's a chew toy." I stood and studied the layout of the stones. "Looking at where everyone is positioned, I don't think Penny or Eddie can be suspects. The angle the arrows came from is wrong. And although the arrows were moving so fast that I didn't see them clearly, they definitely came from the right-hand side of the range."

"It's possible Eddie's a fast mover," Campbell said.

"He was certainly trying to be with Penny."

"I don't mean in that sense. I'm aware of his interest in Penny. He could have jogged into position, killed Ben, then headed back and emerged in a different place to throw us off his trail."

"He'd need to be Olympic style fast. That's quite a distance to cover. We're also looking for a skilled archer."

"Someone as good as Princess Alice," Campbell said.

I looked over at him. "I have to ask again, why are you telling me all this?"

He huffed out a breath. "To make sure you don't get yourself killed. You've risked your neck before to solve a murder. This killer has the ability to shoot deadly arrows from a long distance. That makes you vulnerable."

I looked around the rustling trees, worry crawling up my spine like a giant arachnid with fangs. His words weren't reassuring, but I wasn't backing off. "You're trying to keep me safe?"

"It looks like it. You and the family."

"Does that make us friends if you're watching out for me?"

"How about it doesn't make us enemies?"

I chuckled. "I can live with not being your enemy."

"It's safer for you if you aren't," he said. "Come this way. Let's see how fast a person needs to be to get in the right place to shoot Ben."

I jogged along behind him until we were at the back of the shooting range. "The ground back here makes it hard to move fast. There are all sorts of trip hazards." I kicked a rotting tree stump.

Campbell nodded as he looked around. "Start running."

I stared at him. "You want me to run?"

"Run from here to the other side of the shooting range. I'll time you and see how long it takes."

"We're re-enacting Eddie's movements?"

"Have a detective's badge for figuring that out." A sharp smile crossed his face. "If you want to be involved in this investigation, you need to start running. Investigations always involve some beat pounding."

"I'm not in my running clothes."

"Which is even better," Campbell said. "Eddie was wearing jeans and hiking boots."

My gaze narrowed. "Why don't you run?"

"I'm in charge of the timing." He tapped his wrist watch.

"You can check the time and run," I said. "Besides, you're more Eddie's build. It makes more sense if you run, and I time you."

He grunted. "Not happening."

I crossed my arms over my chest. "I'll run if you do."

Campbell rolled his shoulders. "I'm always up for a challenge, not that you'll be much of one."

I gritted my teeth and twisted my head from side to side. I wasn't going to let him beat me. I could run fast if I needed to. I was especially motivated by the smug look on Campbell's face. "Let's do this."

"Ready in three, two, one. Go." Campbell shot in front of me, but I was right on his heels as we raced past the back of the shooting range.

I dug in and pumped my arms to close the gap. If I let him win this race, I'd never hear the end of it.

Campbell was still ahead of me as we approached the end of the shooting range.

I leaped over a fallen tree and continued to run, my breath gasping out of me and my thighs burning.

"Come on, Holly. You're better than that."

I sucked in a deep breath, ignoring the pounding in my head as I raced to catch up with him.

My foot caught in a root, and I yelped. My arms flailed in front of me. I slammed to the ground and let out an oomph of surprise.

Before I had a chance to roll over, Campbell was by my side. He yanked me up by the back of my shirt. "Everything okay?"

"I'm fine," I grumbled. "I've just proven how difficult it would be to run fast and not hurt yourself back here."

"Are you injured?" His gaze ran over me.

"My foot hurts a bit where I caught it in the root, but nothing's broken."

"I was doing just fine with the terrain." He stepped back and grinned. "And I think this makes me the winner."

"You won by default."

"We can go again. I'll always beat you."

I scowled at him, his smug tone rankling me. "Yes, there's no one in this world quite like you."

"And don't you forget it." He looked around the trees. "Eddie isn't the killer. You'd need to be Ironman fit to get to the right location, make the kill, and conceal your actions. He's not that good."

I nodded as I got my breath back. "So, we're ruling both Eddie and Penny out of the investigation?"

"That's right. That's exactly what I'm doing." He plucked a leaf off my shirt.

I glared at him. "Eddie's still not a nice guy. He doesn't know how to treat women properly. And he did rough up Ben."

"I'm not disagreeing with you on those points. The man's a thug and a bully. He's been spoken to about his behavior. He's learned his lesson."

"I suppose that's something," I said. "But if it wasn't Eddie or Penny, who do you have at the top of your list of suspects?"

"Boss, are you out here?" Drayton's voice drifted toward us.

"Over here." Campbell strode over as Drayton appeared around the side of the shooting range.

"I saw you come out this way," Drayton said. "We've got a new lead on the case."

I hurried over and joined them. "What is it? Has someone confessed?"

Drayton glanced at me and then back to Campbell, surprise in his eyes.

"Don't say a word," Campbell said.

"Hold on a second, I'm involved in this now," I said. "You just showed me around the crime scene. You've gotten me hooked on this mystery."

"Then unhook yourself," Campbell said.

"I can't. Tell me what lead you have," I said. "I've spoken to some of the suspects. I could have vital information to help close this case."

"Which you would have shared with me if you considered it vital information. After all, you want this murder solved as quickly as possible," Campbell said. "I trust you're not withholding valuable information."

"I wouldn't do that," I said. "But you should share with me, too. You know I can help."

"What I need you to do is stay safe," Campbell said. "I brought you out here to show just how risky this case is. There are still plenty of suspects. What's to say they won't make a move to stop you nosing around and revealing their identity?"

"If that's true, then you're also at risk," I said. "You're working to reveal the killer."

"I can look after myself."

"So can I."

"Yes, I've seen how well you take care of yourself in the past."

I glowered at him. "Who's your prime suspect? I can always keep out of their way."

He shook his head. "No more poking around. Keep out of everyone's way, mine included."

"You can't think it was Professor Stephen." I followed along behind Campbell and Drayton as they walked into the clearing. "He's injured, and his wife was with him when Ben was shot. I don't consider either of them suspects."

Drayton shook his head. "It's not—"

"I told you, not a word," Campbell said as he silenced Drayton.

"That only leaves Marcel or Johann," I said. "It has to be one of them. They were in the right place and they both know how to shoot. What information have you got about them? Have either of them got criminal pasts? Or maybe there was trouble with Ben."

"Hold those thoughts." Campbell lifted a finger and pressed it to his ear. "Go ahead, beta team. Over."

I tapped my foot on the ground as I waited for the one-sided conversation to end.

"Confirmed. We're heading back to the castle now. Over."

"Was that about the murder investigation?" I asked.

"Enough, Holly. Get back to the kitchen and forget about this," Campbell said. "You've poked around too much." He turned and walked away with Drayton, leaving me alone in the clearing.

I scowled at his back. It was so typical of Campbell to use me like this. I should learn my lesson when it came to him. He only got me involved when he wanted something out of me, then dropped me like a hot stone.

But I wasn't done yet. I'd find out who killed Ben, and I'd do it before Campbell figured it out. That would wipe the smug look off his face.

A branch cracked behind me, and I jumped and spun around. I hurried back past the shooting range and peered around the edge, Campbell's words of warning bouncing in my head.

Johann appeared in the distance, looking a little worse for wear as he staggered to the side and leaned against a tree.

Was he trying to sneak away? Had he seen us poking around the crime scene and hidden from us? Or had he been watching what we'd been doing and was worried we'd found a clue that implicated him in Ben's murder?

I glanced over my shoulder. Campbell and Drayton were long gone. I needed to do this on my own. I had to find out what Johann was up to, and if it had anything to do with what happened to Ben.

.

Chapter 11

I tiptoed after Johann as I followed him through the trees. From the way he weaved about, he'd been enjoying the contents of his hip flask again.

As I got nearer, he was muttering to himself. From the state he was in, I was confident that if this conversation took a wrong turn, I could outrun him. A gust of wind would knock him over, he was so wobbly.

"Johann, is everything okay?" I sped up and raised a hand.

He spun around and almost lost his balance. "Oh! I thought I was out here on my own." His face was lined with tiredness, and his tie hung limply around his neck. His suit looked crumpled, as if he'd slept in it.

"I was out taking a walk. I hope I'm not interrupting a quiet moment." I slowed as I approached him.

"No, I'm not doing anything special." He squinted at me. "You were at the shooting contest. You're the lady with the cakes."

I stuck out my hand. "That's right. I'm Holly."

He shook my hand before scratching his fingers through his already messy hair, making it stand up on top of his head. "Which means you know all about Ben."

"I do. I'm sorry about that. Did you know him well?"

He nodded. "Well enough."

"Did you see anything in the woods that could help the police with the investigation? They're working hard to catch whoever did this."

Johann swallowed and rubbed his chest. "I... no, I didn't see anything. I know nothing about it."

Those words were full of hidden meaning. "Are you certain about that?"

He pulled out his hip flask. He gave it a shake before tossing it into the undergrowth.

"If you know something, you might feel better if you talk about it. You seem worried."

He glanced at me before hanging his head. "I think I killed Ben."

My mouth dropped open and my stomach somersaulted. "You're confessing to shooting Ben with an arrow?"

His shoulders slumped, and he nodded.

"Why did you kill him?" My hand went to the phone in my back pocket.

"I don't exactly remember what happened. I'd had rather a lot to drink that day, and my shots were getting wild. I'm worried that I misfired and hit Ben."

"It was an accident?"

He scrubbed a hand down his face. "Of course. I had no problem with Ben. I didn't want him dead. And... well, my lucky arrow is missing. I'm terrified it's buried in Ben's chest." He sank slowly to his knees and remained there as if waiting for his execution to take place.

This was sounding less like a confession by the second and more like the ramblings of a drunk guy. "Do you remember shooting in Ben's direction that day?"

Johann let out a shaky sigh. "No, but I remember joking with Marcel, and claiming I could hit a distant target. I could have done it and simply not remember shooting the arrow. Would that still be murder? I never meant to hurt him."

"Go back a few steps." I helped him to his feet. "Weren't you looking for your lucky arrow when you went into the trees during the contest?"

He blinked his red-rimmed eyes at me. "That's right."

"Did you find it and keep using it?"

"Um, well, I don't remember." He kicked a foot through the dirt. "No, I don't think so."

"And how many lucky arrows do you have?"

"Just the one. She's my old faithful, and comes with a beautiful red stripe on one side. I made her myself, and she always strikes her target. Well, she does when I haven't had too much to drink. That whole afternoon is fuzzy, but I feel so guilty. I need to find my arrow. Only then can I be certain I didn't hurt Ben."

"How about we look for your arrow together? If we find it, you'll know you didn't shoot Ben. Besides, surely the police would have tested the arrow that killed Ben for evidence."

His forehead wrinkled. "I guess so. That makes sense."

"And if it was your arrow, it would have your fingerprints or DNA evidence on it."

A glimmer of what might be hope crossed his face. "Yes! That's very true."

"So, if they haven't arrested you, then chances are, you had nothing to do with Ben's death."

"Oh! How clever of you. I've been so panicked, I haven't been able to think straight. You'll really help me find the arrow and prove I'm innocent?" Johann stared down at me, his eyes full of tears.

"Of course!" And if I did that, I could cross him off my suspect list.

"I keep going over that afternoon in my head. I'm such an idiot. I'm not always like this, but things have been difficult for me lately."

"Let's solve this difficulty together. Show me the areas you've already looked in. We can rule them out before we start our search." I patted his arm. "We'll find your lucky arrow if it's out here."

After twenty minutes of stumbling around and walking in circles, we'd eliminated half the area behind the shooting range. We began a slow walk across a patch of ground, searching for his missing arrow.

"I'm glad we ran into each other," he said. "The miserable have no other tonic, but only hope. You've proved to be my tonic, today."

I tilted my head. "That's Shakespeare, isn't it?"

He smiled. "That's right. You bake and enjoy the classics?"

"Some of the classics. And I thought the quote was more like, the miserable have no other medicine, but only hope."

"I think you're right." Johann nodded at me. "You know your history?"

"Some eras better than other. Shakespeare isn't a speciality of mine, but I took an extra course about his life and work when I was a student." We walked along beside each other. "I even saw Professor Stephen speak when I was studying history."

"Ah! Our great Professor Stephen. A learned man. Knowledge is the key to success. I believe that quote is right. Benjamin Franklin."

I smiled. "It sounded good to me."

He chuckled and ran a hand down his face. "I can't seem to keep focused. My head has been such a mess since Ben was killed. What started out as an amazing day, ended in tragedy. It was a bit like a Shakespeare play."

"Did Ben help you with your research, as well?"

"No, nothing like that. Stephen is fiercely protective of the brilliant minds he plucks out of his classes to assist him. He always picks the best and brightest because they help him shine." He leaned closer, stumbling as he did so. "In truth, Stephen was jealous of how clever Ben was. That young man was so quick to understand a new concept, and dedicated to his research."

My eyebrows shot up. Professor Stephen was jealous of Ben? "Surely, if Ben was that clever, he'd have been an asset to Professor Stephen. There'd be no need for him to feel jealous."

"Ah! But Ben had youth on his side. He could work all night and not suffer the consequences. Try doing that as a late-middle-aged man, and you soon feel the pain." He patted his jacket pocket before shrugging.

"You don't think Professor Stephen was jealous enough of Ben to want to get rid of him?"

Johann stopped dead, and stared at me. "That's a horribly twisted thought. Although as we both know from reading the wonders of Shakespeare, jealousy is a strong motive for wanting to kill someone. But not Stephen. However…"

"However, what?"

"Well, I'm sure it's nothing, but Stephen has been saying that he's becoming disillusioned with academia. I think he's losing his touch."

"I'm not sure I follow you."

"When you're young, you don't mind taking risks and challenging the establishment," Johann said. "The problems arise once you're an established figure in the historical community. You become a part of the establishment and must toe the line if you want to keep your position."

"And you have to deal with up and coming students debating your work and pressuring you to move aside?" I said.

"Exactly. We don't like to step outside the boundaries of what's already accepted. It makes us look like mavericks and risks our reputation." He shook his head. "To go back to those early days of being a carefree student, when you had nothing to lose by proposing an outrageous theory, or suggesting someone was wrong and then raking over their research. Neither Stephen nor I would dare do that now for fear of losing our positions. It's a difficult line to tread. And I sensed Stephen was frustrated with this predicament."

"It must be hard finding a well-paid job in your field," I said. "I briefly considered studying for an archeology degree, but I couldn't handle the low pay and lack of opportunity to progress."

"A wise choice. History isn't much easier, though. And you always have to keep an eye out. There's always someone younger, who thinks they're smarter than you, waiting to take your job."

"Did Professor Stephen think Ben wanted his job?"

"Ben was fiercely ambitious, but he had a lot of respect for Stephen. I believe he was happy working as his assistant. And he would have learned a lot from him. Although Stephen's not as sharp as he used to be, he still knows his stuff."

"I've always considered Professor Stephen a genius. His books are incredible."

"That's what he loves everyone to tell him, and he's smart enough to publish regularly, that's always a sensible move. And being his assistant, Ben was guaranteed a placement or a teaching position at the end of his studies. It's no bad thing being associated with the great Stephen Maguire."

We walked along in silence for a moment. Could Professor Stephen be involved in this? He'd been injured during the contest, and his wife was his alibi, but something niggled in my mind. Could Ben have been too clever for his own good, and he'd been killed because of it?

"Have the police spoken to you about the shooting?" I asked.

"They have. The police and one of the security chaps from the castle jointly interviewed me after it happened."

"Were you able to give them any useful information? Did you mention your missing lucky arrow?"

He glanced at me, a shrewd look on his face. "You have the mind of a scholar who's trying to solve a puzzle. It's good to have a natural curiosity when you're interested in history. It helps unpick the murkiness of the past and see the truth."

"I take that as a compliment. Most people simply call me nosy," I said.

He chuckled. "There's nothing wrong with that. I didn't have much to tell the police, and I said nothing about my arrow. It was cowardly, I suppose, but I wasn't sure what I'd done that afternoon. I didn't want to make trouble for myself until I was certain."

Was that true, or did Johann have plans to run if the arrow didn't show up?

"Were you with anyone?" I asked.

"Yes, Marcel was helping me look for the arrow. He also assists Stephen with his research. I'm not a big fan of Marcel, though. He's always trying to ingratiate himself with Stephen. Don't get me wrong, he's a hard worker, but not naturally brilliant minded. He has to put in long hours, and still doesn't always keep up."

"You were together the whole time?"

"Not the whole time. Marcel wandered off, but we were only separated for a short amount of time. Although I did have a sit down and close my eyes for a few minutes.

Fresh air always makes me tired. It was literally five minutes, though. Maybe ten. No more."

That didn't make him the most reliable of witnesses. Being drunk and sleepy could mean things slipped past without him noticing, the killer included.

A phone rang in Johann's pocket. He stopped walking and pulled it out. He stared at the display before shoving it back in his pocket without answering it.

"I don't mind if you need to take that," I said.

"No, I don't want to talk to him." His phone rang again. He grimaced as he looked at it. "I don't know how he got this number. I'd better take this, or I won't get any peace." He wandered away as he answered the call.

I kept searching for the arrow while I waited for Johann to return. I didn't sense any malice in him. He was genuinely worried that he'd done something awful and had been too drunk to remember.

I'd seen for myself that he'd been tipsy at the shooting competition. It seemed unlikely that he'd have been able to accurately fire the arrow that killed Ben.

I also couldn't figure out what his motive was. He spoke highly of Ben. He seemed to like him. And although he didn't have the most airtight of alibis, Marcel was with him most of the time. It would have been almost impossible for Johann to fire the arrow, conceal the weapon, then find Marcel and act as if nothing had happened.

I felt confident I could rule Johann out of this investigation.

I slid my foot under a bush and felt around. A long arrow with a red stripe down the side rolled out. I grinned as I bent and picked it up.

I hurried through the trees to find Johann, slowing as his angry tone drifted toward me.

"I've already said, you'll get your money when I have it. You know the situation I'm in. I'm not a wealthy man."

That didn't sound good. Was Johann in debt?

"I'll get you half at the end of the month. That's the best I can do. My circumstances have changed recently."

I clutched the arrow against my chest. Johann seemed in a bad way. Not only was he drinking too much, he had debt problems as well.

"I can't do more than that. You do what you have to do. But a dead man can't pay you back."

My eyes widened. It sounded like someone had just threatened to kill Johann over money he owed them.

His footsteps approached me. I acted as if I was searching for him, and we almost collided as I rounded the tree.

"Holly!" He grabbed my shoulders. "I didn't know you were so close."

"I was looking for you. I found your arrow." I held it up and pasted a smile on my face.

Some of the darkness disappeared from his features. He took the arrow and stroked his fingers along the wood. "That's such a relief. This proves it. I didn't kill Ben."

"The arrow was under a bush this whole time. You're innocent."

He hugged me, and I got a waft of whiskey on his breath. "Thank you so much. You can't believe how much this means to me."

I gently disentangled myself from his clumsy embrace. "You're welcome. Shall we head back to the castle?"

"That's an excellent idea. All this stress is exhausting. I need a long lie down." He patted his pocket. "And a replacement hip flask."

I glanced at him. "I hope you don't think I'm interfering, but I couldn't help overhear the end of your conversation. Is everything okay?"

He waved his hand in the air. "Everything is fine now I have my arrow back. That was just a small personal matter I had to deal with. It's nothing for you to worry about. Although I appreciate your concern."

It sounded a lot more than a small matter to me, but I decided not to push.

As we walked back through the woods, Johann regaled me of his time as a student and all the fun he'd had. I smiled and nodded along with his comments, but my thoughts were elsewhere.

Now Johann was definitely out of the picture, my thoughts turned to Professor Stephen. I'd been so certain his injury meant he couldn't be a suspect, but if he considered Ben a serious threat to his career, maybe he'd done something to remove that threat. Would he have been motivated enough, despite his injury, to shoot Ben? Was that even possible with his back injury? Or had Alice been right all along? Professor Stephen had faked his injury so he'd be eliminated as a suspect in Ben's murder.

I had to test this idea before I could remove Professor Stephen from my list of suspects. And to do that, I needed Alice's help and her awesome shooting skills.

Chapter 12

"Come on, Meatball, we don't have much time." I hurried along the gravel path early the next morning.

I'd planned to meet Alice at the shooting range to test the theory that Professor Stephen could have shot Ben.

Meatball's ears pricked and his tail lifted before he dashed into the trees. A few moments later, I heard a familiar giggle.

Alice emerged from the trees, Meatball cradled in her arms like he was a giant furry baby, his pink tongue poking out of his mouth and his tail whipping from side to side.

"Thanks for coming out so early," I said.

Alice set Meatball on the ground before patting his head. "I never turn down the opportunity to shoot. And if this helps us figure out who killed Ben, so much the better. I can always have a nap later."

After my conversation with Johann, I'd given Alice an update about what I'd learned. She was more than happy to help me test my theory.

"I thought we could use sandbags to represent Ben." I walked beside Alice toward the shooting range. "We'll set them up in the spot he was in when he was shot. Then you go behind the shooting range and see if you can hit the sandbags from that distance."

"That won't be a problem. You give me a target, and I'll hit it." She pursed her lips. "I can't believe you think Professor Stephen could be involved, though. Everyone is in awe of him, you included."

"I'd as good as ruled him out. But after my conversation with Johann, it got me thinking. What if Professor Stephen felt threatened by Ben's cleverness? Ben was in his final year of study, so would have been applying for jobs. Perhaps Professor Stephen saw him as too big a threat and needed to get him out the way."

"Professor Stephen is a history nerd, not a killer."

"There's nothing nerdy about history," I said. "It's a fascinating topic. And I know you enjoy it. You're always going on about your family tree."

"Yes, that's because my family is fascinating," she said. "The other night, I was researching a relative who helped invent eyeglasses."

"I thought the first spectacles were invented in Florence?"

"I have ancestors all over the world. And I didn't say he invented them, I said he helped." She sniffed and strode ahead.

I shrugged. "Fair enough. You have fabulously talented ancestors."

She grinned over her shoulder at me. "I do. Which reminds me, your family tree is long overdue. We're getting that done. I want to know all about you. After all, you're my best friend. We don't have any secrets from each other."

I glanced at her before looking away. My family had a few secrets, and I didn't want to share them with Alice. I didn't need her to think badly about me because of my somewhat dubious family.

"We'll get around to it," I said. "Right now, we have a murder mystery to figure out. Let's get a move on. I don't want anyone to see what we're doing."

"By anyone, you mean Campbell," Alice said. "Don't worry, I slipped out of my room using the secret passageways. As far as security know, I'm still fast asleep in my bed. What a hoot."

"Then we definitely need to get this done quickly. If they discover you're gone, they'll send out a search party. It'll lead straight to us, and we'll get in trouble."

"I won't get in any trouble," she said.

"I will. Campbell loves having a reason to be angry with me."

She grinned. "Then we'd better make sure we don't get caught."

Ten minutes later, the human-sized sandbags were set up in the shooting range, and Alice had been dispatched around the back. We had to guess where the shooter was standing, so she took a few practice shots to see where her arrows landed. She was an incredible shot. No matter where she stood, her arrows lodged in the sandbag.

"Go farther back," I shouted. "I want to see how far away the shooter could have been before they missed Ben."

"I'll move back ten feet." Alice's voice floated toward me. "Stay out of my range. This is getting hard."

I stood to the side of the shooting range with Meatball to make sure we were out of the danger zone. I only had to wait a few seconds before an arrow shot through the air and skimmed the sandbag.

"I reckon that's about the right distance. You almost missed that time," I said.

"That was the wind's fault. A gust blew just as I let my arrow fly," Alice shouted.

Meatball raced over to the sandbag and launched in the air. He grabbed the arrow and pulled it loose before dropping to the ground and shaking it.

"Less of that. Alice won't want your little teeth marks in her expensive arrows." I scooped him and the arrows up before heading into the trees to find Alice.

"How far away from the target were you when you shot that last arrow?" I said as I approached her.

"A hundred and eight feet," she said. "And being this far away is good going to make an accurate shot, especially with a traditional longbow. By their very design, they're not as accurate as modern day bows."

"And how far back were you pulling your bow string? If you had an injured back muscle, would it hurt to use your bow?"

She winced. "Anyone with an injury would be in serious amounts of pain if they tried that shot. I don't think they'd be able to do it. Here, let me show you." She placed an arrow in her bow and pulled the string back. "Notice how my shoulder muscles are tense. You need to engage them and hold them tight, otherwise your aim will be wildly off."

I set Meatball down and focused on Alice's technique. She was right, someone with a muscular injury would struggle to hold the bow the way she was.

Alice let the arrow fly. "If I was injured, I wouldn't be able to concentrate on my aim because the pain would be too intense."

"What if you were really motivated? What if someone was trying to steal your job, and this was the only opportunity you had to get rid of them?"

Alice lowered the bow and shook her head. "Professor Stephen was with his wife. He could barely walk unaided, let alone shoot. It can't be him."

I blew out a breath. "That's what I've been thinking all this time. Now, I'm not so sure."

"Unless... Evelyn covered for him," Alice said. "They are married. Maybe she doesn't want him getting in trouble. People do crazy things to protect their loved ones. Creating a fake alibi isn't such a wild idea."

"We should speak to them both again, double check their movements, and Professor Stephen's injury. And I need to look into just how threatened he was by Ben."

"Good thinking. Since we're here, have we got time to practice a few more shots?" Alice asked. "I'm just getting warmed up, and I can show you how to fire an arrow if you'd like. It's fun."

Meatball barked several times, his ears lifting.

"And Meatball thinks it's an excellent idea," Alice said.

"I'm not sure he's interested in the shooting." His nose was pointed away from the shooting range. "Something's got his attention, though."

"There are tons of pheasants in these woods," Alice said. "Maybe he's picked up on the scent of one."

Meatball bounced on his paws a few times before giving an excited yip and racing away.

"Stop! Meatball." I looked at Alice. "We'd better catch him. We don't want him bothering the wildlife."

"He's no match for a pheasant," Alice said as we hurried along behind Meatball. "They're big birds. If a couple gang up on him, he won't stand a chance."

"Meatball may be small, but he's mighty," I said. "Never underestimate a small dog when he's determined to do something."

More barking drifted toward us. I tilted my head. That didn't sound like Meatball. As I listened, several more barks started up, and my stomach dropped.

"The Duchess's corgis must be out for their morning walk." I sped up. Things never ended well when Meatball encountered the household corgis.

"It's a bit early for them to be out," Alice said. "Ooh, look! Giant fungi. Rupert will be so jealous I've found these. They must be the first of the year. I'm taking a picture to send him."

"You enjoy the fungi, I'll find Meatball."

The barking grew louder as I hurried past a large row of fir trees. I discovered Meatball in a stand-off with three snapping corgis. I looked around but saw no sign of anyone with them.

"That's enough, you guys," I said. "Meatball, heel."

He took a step back to me, his hackles raised and a grumble rumbling in his chest.

The three corgis barked and advanced on him.

"There they are." Marcel jogged into view, his cheeks bright pink, and two more corgis with him. "These three slipped their leashes. I've been looking for them for ages."

"Hi, Marcel. You're walking the Duchess's dogs?" I kept my attention on Meatball and the corgis so I could step in if a fight broke out.

"Do you have a problem with that?" Marcel made a grab for one of the loose corgis.

"No, it's just that they have a dog walker who takes them out when the Duchess is busy. I'm surprised to see you with them."

"I saw the Duchess yesterday and offered to help. She was only too happy to let me borrow her dogs." Marcel grimaced as he almost lost his grip on another leash. "I didn't realize they'd be such a handful, though. I figured they'd be well-trained. They're a nightmare."

"They can be tricky to handle," I said. "It comes with their regal status." The corgis loved to bully Meatball, which was why I always tried to keep them separated.

Marcel tried to slip a leash on one of the corgis, but it dodged out of his way and circled behind Meatball.

"They don't like that dog much," Marcel said. "Is he yours?"

"Yes, this is Meatball. They're definitely not friends. I don't think the corgis like him because he's a crossbreed. They're snobs."

Marcel's eyebrows shot up. "Dogs don't think like that. They're not clever enough."

"These definitely are," I said. "They go out of their way to be mean to him."

Meatball whirled around as one of the corgis got too close and issued a warning growl.

"Come here, you lot," Marcel said. "No picking on the poor mutt."

I frowned. Meatball may be a mutt, but he was a fabulous one.

Marcel tried to grab one of the corgis again, but it danced away, a smug look on its furry face. "Wretched things. Why do they have to be so difficult?"

"Did you bring any dog treats?" I said. "They always respond to food."

"Oh! I didn't think to do that. I don't suppose you've got any?"

I always had treats in my jacket pocket when I walked Meatball. It was a sure-fire way of getting him to follow commands. Well, most of the time. "Try these." I handed Marcel a dozen treats.

He waved them under the corgis' noses. "This way, you beasts. Let's go back to the castle."

The corgis' evil intentions remained fixed on Meatball. They were determined to have a showdown.

"They don't like your food," he said. "I'm going to make a grab for them. Once I get the leashes on, they'll be under my control."

Marcel clearly didn't know dogs that well. These corgis were never under anyone's control unless they wanted to be.

I stuffed a treat under Meatball's nose. While he was distracted by eating it, I gathered him into my arms and out of the way of the evil intent glinting in the beady eyes of the circling dogs.

My timing was perfect. The corgis barked furiously as their rival was taken away. Marcel lunged at a corgi and landed on his knees with a grunt, missing his target.

A particularly plump corgi jumped up at his face, while another landed on his back.

"Argh! They're attacking me," Marcel yelled.

"I don't think they'll bite you," I said, although I wouldn't put it past them. "They think you're playing."

Marcel was knocked on his face as two more corgis joined in the rough play.

"What's going on?" Alice appeared and stared down at Marcel.

"Princess Alice! I didn't know you were out here, too." Marcel tried to get to his feet but was knocked down by a corgi barrel rolling into his knees.

I stepped away and stood next to Alice as the corgis ran circles around Marcel.

"Do you think we should help him?" I whispered.

"In a couple of minutes," she said. "This is fun to watch."

"You're a good boy," I said to Meatball. "You'd never do anything so mean."

He licked my cheek, and I fed him another treat.

"You take care of Meatball." I handed him to Alice. "I'll deal with this rambunctious lot." I strode over, snagged the leashes out of Marcel's hand, and dodged around, clipping them on the corgis and slowly getting them back in some semblance of order.

Marcel rolled away and jumped to his feet, his clothes covered in dirt and leaves. "Those animals are uncontrollable. How does the Duchess manage them?"

"They're her babies." I passed him the leashes. "She lets them run a bit wild. They're better behaved when they're around her. They know who the boss is."

"I'd never have offered to take them if I'd known they'd be like this." He frowned down at the yapping corgis. "I suppose, I should thank you."

"You're very welcome," I said.

His gaze went to Alice, and his cheeks flushed. "It's nice to see you again, Princess."

She smiled as she stroked Meatball. "You, too. Although I shouldn't be speaking to you, since you tried to have me disqualified from the shooting contest."

He winced. "Please, don't take it personally, but I believe rules are there to be followed. Women didn't shoot in medieval times. That's not to say you weren't very good with your longbow. Have you been out practicing this morning?" His gaze went to her bow.

"Something like that," Alice said. "You weren't a bad shot yourself during the contest."

"I'm one of the best in the history department." Marcel brushed leaves off his sweater and puffed out his chest.

"Better than Professor Stephen?" I asked.

"He's a decent shot, but he's getting on a bit. And we all saw him get injured."

"What about Ben?" I asked. "Did you think he was a good shot?"

Marcel's gaze narrowed as he looked from Alice and back to me. "Ben was good at everything."

"Was it hard to keep up with him?" I asked. "Everyone I've spoken to about Ben told me how clever he was. It must have gotten annoying being around someone so brilliant."

Marcel shrugged. "Not really. And I have an IQ of one hundred and forty, so I'm equally as clever. I mean, sure, there was some competition between us, but it was friendly enough. That's how things are. There's never enough funding for the work we all want to do. We have to fight to keep our places. We understood that."

"I'm assuming the police spoke to you about what happened that day," I said.

"What if they did?" Marcel lifted his chin. "I don't like the implication of that comment."

"Holly can imply anything she likes. She's my right-hand woman. You'd be wise to answer her questions," Alice said.

He sniffed before shrugging. "Of course, Princess. I expect the police have spoken to both of you, anyway, since you were there. You already know what happened."

"Holly actually saw the arrow that hit Ben," Alice said.

Marcel grimaced. "That can't have been pleasant."

"I expect it wasn't pleasant for Ben, either," I said. "You were with Johann when it all happened. Is that right?"

Marcel scratched the back of his head. "Most of the time. I already told the police this."

"I'd love to hear it from you directly. Why don't you tell us?" Alice's smile was saccharine sweet.

He bobbed his head. "As you wish, Princess. I did separate from Johann when we were behind the shooting range."

"Was he acting oddly when you were with him? Trying to get rid of you?" I asked.

"No, nothing like that." He adjusted the leashes in his hands. "Although I've been worried about him for some time. If the police are still looking for someone to blame, I suggest they speak to Johann again. He was acting like an idiot that day. He'd been drinking and was firing his arrows without knowing where they'd land. That was dangerous. I told him to be more careful, but he just laughed. He said he had nothing left to worry about. The worst had already happened to him."

That wasn't quite the way Johann had described things to me. He'd seemed mortified that he may have accidentally shot Ben. "Did you see him fire an arrow at Ben?"

"No, but he could have done it when I wasn't with him," Marcel said. "The man has a serious drinking problem. It's only gotten worse since his wife left him. His life is falling apart. And he's in debt up to his ears. You don't get a king's ransom working at the university."

"Just because he's struggling with money, that's not a reason to kill Ben," I said.

"I never said he killed him," Marcel said. "But he didn't know what he was doing that afternoon. He'd had three large brandies before we even went outside, and I know he had at least one hip flask tucked in his jacket. I feel sorry for the guy. He was once an amazing lecturer. He's had six books published. Now, he's a laughing stock. It's only a matter of time before he gets fired. That is, if the police don't arrest him."

"You shouldn't accuse someone unless you have actual evidence," Alice said.

"I'm not, but it's the logical conclusion," Marcel said. "Johann was drunk and in control of a deadly weapon."

"Have you told the police this theory?" I asked.

"Of course. They're looking into it," he said. "I really must get back with these corgis, before one of them bites me."

Alice adjusted her hold on Meatball and lifted a finger. "Wait, a moment. Are you done, Holly?"

Marcel glowered at me but remained in place.

"Yes, that's it," I said, struggling to keep my expression neutral. It was fun to see Marcel squirm.

He opened his mouth as if to ask a question, then simply nodded at Alice. "It's always a pleasure." He turned and left, the corgis yapping and tugging on their leashes as they disappeared back into the trees.

"I don't like him," Alice said. "Marcel was very quick to point the finger at Johann and highlight his problems. I feel sorry for Johann. He's drinking too much, his wife has left him, and he has money worries. He doesn't want a manslaughter charge added to that."

"Johann is in a bad place," I said. "And I overheard a conversation he had that suggested the money problems are real. But I don't think he killed Ben. Marcel confirmed that by letting on just how drunk Johann was that day."

"Of course! You don't drink and shoot. Being even a tiny bit tipsy impairs distance vision."

"Where did you learn that, Professor Alice?"

She nudged me with her hip. "I remember things I'm passionate about. Could Marcel be the shooter? He's using Johann's misfortune to take the attention off him. He just painted us a picture of a desperate, broken man with nothing going for him."

"Marcel's on the suspect list and moving up fast."

"And he's so fake. I bet he was only walking the corgis to get on the right side of the Duchess," Alice said. "I could tell he didn't like them. And he was all smarmy around me. People get like that when they're in the presence of a princess."

"You do dazzle some people with your high class ways and fancy castle living."

She tipped back her head and laughed. "Have I ever dazzled you?"

"Oh, Princess. You dazzle me every day."

"Ha, ha. What's our next move?" She pressed a kiss on Meatball's head.

"We keep an eye on Marcel. If his rivalry with Ben wasn't friendly, that gives him a motive. I also want to talk to Professor Stephen and make sure he was genuinely injured during the shooting contest. If I can find out more about his injury and how bad it was, that should rule him out."

"Then we can focus on finding proof that Marcel killed Ben."

I nodded. "First, we question Professor Stephen, then we tackle Marcel."

Chapter 13

I was hard at work in the kitchen and had spent most of the day baking and filling cherry cream pies, whipping and icing vanilla sponge cakes, and kneading a mountain of bread.

I looked up as the kitchen door opened. Betsy Malone bustled in, her cheeks bright pink.

"Afternoon, Betsy," I said. "You're timing is perfect. I've got a batch of sugar cookies cooling."

She rubbed her hands together and smiled at me. "That's just what I need. I've had quite a day. Two of my regular girls called in sick this morning, so I've been covering for them. I've only just finished the cleaning. I'm normally home by now with my feet up and a large gin by my side. Purely for medicinal purposes, you understand." Betsy looked after a team of dedicated cleaners who made sure the castle was kept immaculate.

"Sit down. I'll get you a cup of tea and some cookies. I need to give my arms a rest from all this dough pounding." I finished with my bread before placing it in the warming cabinet to rise. I made the tea and plated up some cookies, then sat opposite her at the kitchen table.

"Thank you." She took a big sip of tea. "I'm glad I ran into you. I've been hearing all about what happened at the shooting contest the other day."

"I imagine that tragedy is all over the village," I said. Most likely aided along by Betsy and her friends. Even though she claimed not to, Betsy loved a good gossip.

"I've heard mention of it just about everywhere," Betsy said. "Do the police have any ideas who did it?" She dunked a sugar cookie in her tea.

"There are a few suspects," I said. "In fact, I was there when it happened, but I'm trying to keep out of it."

She chuckled. "Of course you are. It's not like you to go around investigating a mystery."

I grinned. "I like to see justice served. There's no harm in that. It's not right that crimes go unpunished."

"I'm behind you there." Betsy glanced around before leaning closer. "Did the arrow really go straight through that unfortunate man's chest?"

I grimaced as I grabbed a sugar cookie. "It did. He died straight away."

"Well, at least he didn't suffer," Betsy said. "There's nothing worse than a lingering death. What a terrible way to go, though. And since the police don't seem to be getting anywhere, have you got any idea who killed him?"

I tilted my head from side to side. "I've got one or two thoughts on the matter."

She patted my hand. "I knew you would. Tell me everything."

"I've no proof about any of this. I'm just guessing what could have happened. But I was hoping to speak to Professor Stephen Maguire today. Ben was his assistant. He may have some ideas about who'd want to kill him." Or he could even be involved, but I wasn't sharing that with Betsy or it would be front page news tomorrow.

A frown marred her face. "If you're referring to that posh guy complaining about his back in the guest wing, you want to stay away from him."

"Why do you say that?"

"I was in his room, sorting out the bathroom, which was a right mess, dirty towels everywhere. He yelled at me to get out. I told him I was only doing my job, but he said he needed to relax and not be bothered by the likes of me. Whatever could he mean by that? I'm always discreet when I do my work. I'm known for my discretion."

I stifled a grin. "You absolutely are. No one cleans a bathroom like you do."

"Less of your cheek." She swatted the back of my hand. "Anyway, after he was so rude, he had the cheek to order me to bring in extra towels to use during his masseuse appointment. She was going in the room just as I was leaving."

"He must be trying to help his back. He got injured when he was shooting."

"I couldn't give two figs about his back. It's his bad manners that need working on. You can always tell a person's true character by the way they treat the wait staff and the cleaners."

I nodded. If Professor Stephen was faking his injury, he was pulling out all the stops to make it look genuine.

"It's funny, though." Betsy took another cookie. "I saw the masseuse leave not long after she'd arrived. She looked very pale and was clutching her stomach. I expect she got yelled at as well and walked out. It would serve him right if she did. Manners cost nothing."

"Maybe I should go up and see him. Make sure everything is okay. Professor Stephen could be in a bad mood because of his back injury. Pain can make people short-tempered. That could be why he snapped at you."

"You be careful, young Holly. You don't want to get in trouble by poking around in a murder investigation."

"I'm not poking, simply finding a way to learn useful information that could stop a killer from getting away with a horrible crime."

"Same difference." She ate another cookie. "Just be prepared to get yelled at if you do see him."

"I could try sweetening him up," I said. "Professor Stephen ate several pieces of the gingerbread I made for the shooting contest. I could take some with me when I check in on him."

"And that's the only reason you want to speak to him?" Betsy arched an eyebrow. "Or do you think he's involved in this murder?"

"I'm just covering all the bases," I said. "I've no proof Professor Stephen was involved."

From the shrewd look on Betsy's face, she didn't believe me. "Hmmm. Prodding at a murder suspect seems reckless. I could come with you if you think he's dangerous. I could squirt him in the face with my polish if he gets mean. I was tempted to do just that when he was so rude to me."

"I'll be fine. And you've had a busy day. Stay here and finish the sugar cookies and tea." I was already on my feet, plating up some gingerbread. "I'll go see Professor Stephen for five minutes. Which room is he in?"

"Third room on the left in the guest wing. Don't let him be rude to you like he was to me."

"Thanks, Betsy. I won't." I checked to make sure Chef Heston wasn't around to see me sneaking off, before hurrying out of the kitchen.

I headed up the stairs to the bedroom and knocked on the door.

"Come in," Professor Stephen said, his voice sounding muffled.

I opened the door an inch, pausing as I almost lost my grip on the plate of gingerbread.

"It's about time," he said. "You told me the other girl was only fifteen minutes away."

I pushed the door open wider, and my mouth dropped open. Professor Stephen was on his front on a fold out massage table, with two large white towels covering him.

"Come in. I'm in desperate need of this massage," he said. "And I expect a discount for being made to wait so long."

"There's been a misunder—"

"And that other girl had better not have been contagious. She sneezed twice before making her excuses and leaving."

My mouth opened and closed several times. "I, um…"

"Stop stuttering and do your job," Professor Stephen said. "I'm in pain. Start rubbing me."

I licked my lips as I placed the gingerbread down and stepped closer to the table. "Professor Stephen, this is a bit of a—"

"If I have to tell you to do your job one more time, I'll make sure this is the last job you actually have."

Although the last thing I wanted to do was rub the flesh of a man I barely knew, this gave me the perfect chance to question him. And if he got mean, I could always poke his sore spots.

I glanced at the closed door. This was a risk. The replacement masseuse would be on her way. I didn't have much time. It was either grab the bottle of oil by the table and ask a few questions about Ben's murder, or run.

I cautiously lifted the top of the white towel covering Professor Stephen's shoulders and was grateful that he didn't have a hairy back. "I'll start at the top and work down."

"Fine. Just get a move on," he said.

I squeezed sandalwood infused oil onto my hands and began a tentative massage of his right shoulder.

"Use much more pressure," Professor Stephen said. "I can barely feel that."

"Of course," I said, hoping he wouldn't recognize my voice. "You said you're in pain. How were you injured?"

He lifted his head, but I grabbed the back of his neck and kept him in place, making sure it remained in the hole at the top of the massage table. "It's best if you don't move."

"Oh, very well. I suppose you know what you're doing." His head lowered back into the hole. "I hurt my back when I was out shooting."

"With a gun?"

"No, with a longbow. It's an ancient medieval weapon you may not be familiar with. I was leading the contest but decided to go for a final bullseye and secure a conclusive win."

I smirked and shook my head. He hadn't been leading the contest. "That sounds exciting. What happened?"

"I was lining up a difficult shot. I was focused on the target, when I felt a muscle go in my lower back. The pain shot up my back and then down my leg. I couldn't continue the contest. Can you massage lower? That's where the pain is worse."

I replaced the towel over his shoulder and folded it in half to reveal his lower back.

"Is this the first time you've had a back injury like this?" I asked.

"I've had a few problems in the past," he said. "Nothing like this, though. Please, massage lower. It's my right buttock that's the real problem."

My fingers froze, and I pressed my lips together. I wasn't massaging his backside. "You must have incredible skills if you can fire a longbow. Is it difficult to learn how to shoot one?"

"Very difficult. You need to be strong. As you can see, I have excellent muscle tone, so it's no problem for me."

I hummed in what I hoped sounded like agreement. He looked a little on the flabby side.

"I'm an expert in a number of ancient weapons," he said. "They're all difficult to learn. You have to practice for hours to become proficient. I usually win the competitions I enter."

"How exciting," I said. "I hope you don't mind me asking, but I heard talk that there was a tragedy at a recent shooting contest. Were you there?"

He was silent for a few seconds. "I figured word would get out about this. Yes, I was at that contest. It happened in the castle grounds. The chap who died was my assistant."

"I'm so sorry for your loss," I said.

"I appreciate that. Please, massage lower."

I inched my fingers down his back but couldn't face touching his buttock cheek. "Did you see what happened?"

"No, he was shot just after I got injured."

"And the victim worked with you?"

"That's right."

"What sort of work do you do?"

"I'm a senior historical lecturer at King's College."

"Wow! You're not only amazing at using weapons, but clever, too."

He chuckled. "You're very kind. And astute for a masseuse."

My nostrils flared, but I kept on rubbing. "What about the victim? Could he shoot?"

"Yes, Ben was good with a longbow. And he was an incredible student. I only ever pick the brightest students to mentor. Ben was going places. I'm not sure I'll find anyone as good as him. He's a real loss to the academic world."

"And a loss to you, I imagine," I said. "If you mentored him, you must have known him well."

"I always ensure there are professional boundaries with my students. It's not good to let them get too attached. They expect too much. But I liked having him around. Go lower with your fingers." He gestured to his buttock cheek. "Get right into the fleshy part."

I grimaced and lowered the towel covering his buttock an inch. A hairy round cheek revealed itself. I couldn't hold off from this hideous task any longer.

"Ah. That's it. You're in the right spot at last."

I looked anywhere but at Professor Stephen's backside. This was so weird. I'd seen this man give an informed lecture on Tudor law and now had his naked pink body on display to me.

"Was Ben a popular student?" I asked. "I expect there'll be lots of people who'll miss him."

"He was a popular guy, but there'll be less tension in the department now he's gone."

"Oh! Did he have problems with someone?"

"More pressure on my buttock."

I dug in with a thumb, and Professor Stephen jumped. "How's that?"

"Better," he squeaked. "Be careful. You're right on the tender bit."

"That must have been stressful for you, if there were problems in your department. Stress is bad for muscular pain. Was it a problem with another lecturer?"

He let out a sigh. "No, nothing like that. I have another assistant, and they weren't friendly. Marcel was always hassling Ben. It was tedious having to keep them apart."

"Why didn't they like each other?"

"I, um, well, I never asked. Unlike you, I didn't ask them a lot of questions about private matters."

"I find my clients like to talk when they're relaxing. Speaking to a stranger can be soothing. No judgment, you see."

"Hmm, I suppose so. Marcel's problem was most likely professional jealousy. And recently, they'd been going after the same pot of grant money, so the tension in the department was worsening. Ben was always the better student, though. I keep Marcel around because he's so eager to please. I like having someone at my beck and call."

That didn't match with what Marcel had told me. It sounded like Marcel had targeted Ben and made his life difficult.

This new information gave Marcel a great motive for murder. If he wanted to be number one in Professor Stephen's eyes and was chasing a pot of money only one of them would get, he'd definitely want Ben out of the way.

"Is there a problem? You've stopped," Professor Stephen said.

"Sorry! I was just resting my hands."

"Do you have time to do a full body massage?" Professor Stephen asked.

A full body massage? The idea sent a shudder down my spine. I flipped the towel over his lower half and stepped away from the table. "No, I must go. I have another client."

"I'm happy to pay extra," Professor Stephen said. "Let me flip over, and you can get to work. I've got a lot of tension in my groin area."

"I wish I could help, but I need to be somewhere else." I turned away as Professor Stephen struggled onto his side so he wouldn't see my face, and I wouldn't see his, well, I didn't even want to imagine what would be on display.

"I could do with some help. My injury makes it hard for me to turn," Professor Stephen said. "Oh, hold on a second. I think I've got it."

I risked a glance just as the towel covering Professor Stephen's lower half slid off. I grabbed the towel, closed my eyes, and flung it at his head. "If you'll excuse me. I'll be leaving now."

"Wait! You haven't finished."

I raced out the room and shut the door behind me. I shook my head, my heart thudding. What had I been thinking, posing as a masseuse? If Professor Stephen had gotten a good look at my face, I'd have been in trouble.

I rested my head against the door. At least I'd gotten some interesting information. Ben and Marcel hadn't been friends. Marcel had lied to me.

I turned and slammed straight into someone. My oily hands landed on their chest. I bounced away with a startled oomph.

Campbell glared down at me before looking at his oil-stained shirt. "Care to explain what's going on here?"

I hid my hands behind my back. "That wasn't my fault. You're always sneaking up on me."

"I never sneak." He lifted an eyebrow. "What were you doing in Professor Stephen's room? And why do you smell like you've just spent a week on some hippie retreat?"

I glanced back at the closed door. "I'm not sure you'd believe me if I told you."

A woman dressed in a white tunic and pants approached. "Is this Professor Stephen Maguire's room?"

I nodded as I stepped to the side to get out of her way. "That's right."

"I hope he's not in a bad mood. My colleague was taken ill, and I'm covering for her. I got here as quickly as I could."

"I'm sure he'll be thrilled you're here. He's waiting for you," I said.

"Thanks." She knocked on the door before hurrying in and closing it behind her.

When I turned back and risked a glance at Campbell, he was smirking.

"I'm going to love to hear your explanation for this."

Chapter 14

I'd been caught red-handed by Campbell, snooping where I shouldn't. Well, my hands were covered in sandalwood infused oil, but it was the same thing.

"Come on, Holly, don't keep me in suspense. What are you up to?" Campbell said.

"Nothing bad."

"You bolted out of Professor Stephen's room like you were about to get caught doing something you shouldn't."

I lifted my chin. "I needed to speak to him. I wasn't sure if he'd been genuinely injured during the shooting competition."

Campbell sniffed the air. "Fragrant oil, a guilty look on your face, and a late running masseuse. Did you give Professor Stephen a rub down to check his back injury?"

"Um, well, that wasn't what I'd planned to do."

He snorted a laugh. "You impersonated someone else. That's a crime."

My cheeks grew warm. "My intentions were good. They started out with gingerbread and descended into something horrific involving oil and a hairy buttock cheek that will give me nightmares."

Campbell took hold of my arm and escorted me away from the bedroom and along the corridor. "Keep talking."

There was no way I was getting out of this. "I thought I could get him to open up if I brought him some food. When I got to his room and went in, he was lying naked on a massage table. He thought I was the replacement masseuse."

"And you decided not to correct him?"

"I was going to, but he started barking orders, so I played along. I figured if he was nice and relaxed, he'd talk to me."

"Unbelievable. And did he?"

"If you keep being mean, I'm not sharing anymore."

"This isn't mean. This is me keeping a lid on my anger and not reporting you to the police for deception."

"It wasn't a deception, it was—"

"Being a trouble maker. Go on."

I huffed out a breath. "Professor Stephen bragged a bit about how amazing he was with a longbow, but he also told me something interesting about Marcel."

"Which was?"

"Marcel lied to me," I said.

"About his whereabouts at the time of the murder?" Campbell's eyes narrowed. "He was collecting arrows with Johann. They both confirmed that in their statements."

"Not about that. Did they also tell you they separated when they were in the woods?"

Campbell glanced out a window we passed, his mouth set in a firm line.

"Hey, if I'm sharing, then you need to," I said.

"I didn't say I wasn't sharing."

"You're not exactly talkative."

"You share first."

I did want to talk this through with someone, even if that someone considered me an annoyance. "Marcel highlighted the fact they got separated when they were looking for arrows. He also made it clear that Johann had been drunk during the contest. He suggested that Johann accidentally shot Ben."

"I'm assuming that when you questioned Johann, which, of course, you've already done, he refuted this?"

There was no point in hiding my snooping activities from Campbell. "Not so much. He confirmed they got separated, but only for a short amount of time. Johann was concerned he may have accidentally killed Ben, but he didn't. We found the arrow he thought may have been the murder weapon. He was so relieved. Actually, I feel a bit sorry for Johann. The guy's a mess."

Campbell nodded as we continued along the corridor and down the stairs. "Johann has debt problems. We've looked into his background. He's about to go under. His wife left him and took the house and most of the assets. Johann was living in his car until that was repossessed. He's a desperate man."

"Desperate enough to kill Ben?" I asked. "I can't figure out what Johann's motive is. Maybe Marcel is trying to make Johann the fall guy for something he did."

"We haven't found a motive for Johann, either," Campbell said.

"You should talk to Marcel again."

"Thanks for the advice."

"I'm serious. He's sneaky. I didn't take to him when we talked. Neither did Princess Alice."

Campbell glared at me. "You're involving the Princess in your snooping?"

"No." My voice rose an octave. "Only a little. And not deliberately. She was with me when we met Marcel in the woods. She got involved by accident."

"What were you doing in the woods? Did she have an escort with her?"

"No, because this isn't the eighteenth century, and women are allowed to walk in the woods on their own."

"Not when there's an arrow slinging killer on the loose. I shall have to speak to my security team. Princess Alice is vulnerable."

"She's also a crack shot who can run rings around any of your guys with a longbow."

"That's hardly the point."

"Your security isn't to blame," I said. "You know Princess Alice can be inventive when she wants to do something."

Campbell sucked air through his teeth. "She used the passageways in the castle to get out, didn't she?"

"I'm sworn to secrecy."

He grunted and strode ahead of me.

I hurried to keep up with him. "So, what are you going to do about Marcel?"

"You still haven't told me what he was being untruthful about."

"Oh! His friendship with Ben," I said. "Marcel claimed they were simply friendly rivals at the university. Professor Stephen just told me the opposite. Marcel didn't treat Ben well. They were also chasing the same grant money. Only one of them was going to get it."

"You think Marcel killed Ben for this money? How much are we talking?"

"I don't know, but it's a theory I'm interested in. And if it's a big amount of money, it may be worth killing over."

"No amount of money is worth killing over."

"You know what I mean. Everyone's going around saying what a golden boy Ben was. Marcel must have hated that, always coming second to him. He could have finally done something about it. He saw the opportunity at the shooting contest and took it."

"It's not a terrible theory."

"Admit it, it's a great theory."

"I'll speak to Marcel again," Campbell said.

"He should be your prime suspect," I said. "He has a motive, he had an opportunity, and he had the means."

"I'm well aware of all of that," Campbell said. "That still doesn't mean I approve of you interrogating suspects behind my back."

"I'm just trying to be helpful."

"Even though I've warned you off because there's a killer on the loose?" He turned and faced me. "What do you get out of this?"

"A huge sense of satisfaction when the killer is caught," I said. And maybe the chance to beat Campbell and show him it wasn't only tough guy alpha males who could solve crimes.

"That's my job."

"Don't say you're threatened by little old me asking a few questions." I smiled up at him.

"You're hardly a threat," he said.

"Then you won't mind me investigating," I said. "If you're so sure you'll find the killer, then I can keep on being nosy."

"Only if you want to find an arrow lodged in your chest," Campbell said.

"Whoever killed Ben won't come after me. This murder feels personal. And if it was Marcel, then he did it to take out a rival. This is linked to their work at the university. It's about a fight to get to the top."

"You've ruled out everyone else?"

"Pretty much. How about you?"

"It's a work in progress. What about Professor Stephen? You think he could be involved?" Campbell asked.

"I didn't, but it was something Princess Alice said that got me thinking. At the shooting contest, she wondered if he faked his injury because he wasn't going to win, but maybe he faked it to take his name off the suspect list."

"I was there. I saw when Professor Stephen's back gave out. Genuine pain crossed his face. I've seen it happen to my team when they're training and a muscle popped. It's like a fire brand stuck through your flesh."

I grimaced. "I agree. Professor Stephen looked in bad shape after he was injured. I had to be sure I could eliminate him from my inquiry."

"You don't have an inquiry," Campbell said.

"Holly! I've been looking everywhere for you." Rupert bounded along the corridor and came to a stop in front of us.

"Lord Rupert." Campbell nodded his head.

He returned the nod. "Have you got the afternoon off work, Holly? I was just in there asking where you were. No one knew."

My heart skipped a beat. I'd been so focused on Professor Stephen that I'd forgotten I should only have left the kitchen for five minutes. "No, and I must get back."

"Let me walk with you," Rupert said.

I glanced at Campbell. "Are we all done?"

"For now," he said. "Just be careful."

"I always am." I smiled at Rupert as I turned away. "Let's go."

"What does Campbell think you need to be careful about?" he asked.

I glanced over my shoulder. Campbell was still watching. "He thinks I don't know how to handle myself."

"Is this about the murder?"

I nodded. "I'm not at any risk. He's being overly cautious."

"I'm glad he is. I don't want you to come to any harm."

"There's zero chance of that. Most people don't notice the castle staff. I have that on my side when I'm investigating. I'm practically invisible."

"Not to me you aren't."

My stomach flipped over, and my cheeks heated. "That's very nice of you to say."

Rupert's cheeks also flared with color. "Alice told me you're looking into what happened to Ben. Have you made any progress?"

"I'm still working on it."

"I hope you won't be too busy to join us tonight."

"Tonight? What's happening?"

"Games night, of course. It's your once a year chance to be waited on by me." Rupert grinned. "It's always such fun when we have to look after the staff."

I smacked my hand against my forehead. "Of course! I'd forgotten all about it." Every week, the staff got together to have a games night. We'd pull out cards and board games, and everyone would join in. Once a year, the Audley family would wait on the staff. And it was happening tonight. It was a tradition that went back hundreds of years.

"Say you'll be there," Rupert said. "I'm sure you can have a night off from this investigation to enjoy yourself."

"I'll definitely be there," I said.

He bowed before opening the door to the kitchen. "Then I shall look forward to serving you, madam."

"I'm so excited about this evening." Louise walked alongside me as we headed to the saloon. The room was usually out of bounds to visitors, so we were privileged to be using it for our games night.

"Me, too. The family always pull out the stops when they're in charge." I smoothed my hand down the smart red dress I'd worn. All the staff got dressed up for this special event. And another bonus about this evening was that we didn't have to cook. The Duchess always ordered in lavish food from an outside caterer.

Mason and Kace stood outside the saloon as we approached. They bowed low, both with smiles on their faces.

"Welcome to games night, ladies," Mason said. "I hope you have a pleasant evening."

"We definitely will," Louise said. "Is Campbell working tonight?"

"He's around." Mason opened the door.

Louise grinned at me. "This dress is new. I was hoping to make a good impression on him."

"You look really beautiful." Louise wore a 1960s-inspired cream dress with a pinched-in waist and a bow at the back. Her hair had been set in pin curls, and her makeup was all big lashes and thick eyeliner.

Most of the staff had already arrived, and there was an excited buzz in the air as I wandered around greeting people and looking at the games that had been set out.

I was deciding on whether to join in a new game of Clue or go for some old-fashioned high card draw, when Alice hurried over.

"I got you something special to wear for this evening." She thrust a box into my hand.

"Another gift?"

"This is only a loan." Alice wore an old-fashioned black-and-white servant's outfit, complete with a white cap and frilly apron.

"Thanks. You didn't need to do that," I said. "I love your outfit. Very Downton Abbey."

"Isn't it fun?" She spun in a circle. "I make a great serving wench."

I laughed. "You absolutely do." I pulled off the box lid, and my mouth fell open.

Alice clapped her hands together. "Do you like it?"

"It's a tiara," I said. The glittering stones sparkled under the chandelier.

"I thought you might like it for the evening. You can be the Castle's princess for the night." Alice lifted it out of the box and settled it on my head before teasing my hair around it.

"It's heavy," I said.

"I always get headaches if I wear a tiara for too long."

"It's not real, is it?" I lifted a hand and touched the cold stones.

Alice giggled. "I'd better go. We're still sorting out the food. Rupert keeps eating it and spoiling the arrangement. He's so greedy." She turned and hurried away.

I looked around the room, my hand still touching the tiara. I needed to grab my spot if I was going to get involved in a game.

My gaze went to the door where Campbell had appeared. He beckoned me over with a finger.

I hurried toward him. "Have you got any useful updates?"

"About what?"

"You know what." I pursed my lips. "Have you spoken to Marcel?"

He tilted his head a fraction. "I like your tiara."

"Thanks. Alice loaned it to me. You don't think it's a bit too much?"

"It's definitely too much. That thing is worth millions."

I grabbed the tiara off my head. "I asked her if it was genuine. I can't wear this all night. I might damage it."

"I'll be keeping an eye on you. No running off with the family jewels."

"I have no plans to run off with the princess's tiara. Maybe you should have it."

He took it from me and set it back on my head. "She loaned it to you in good faith. Princess Alice will be offended if you don't wear it."

Campbell had a point. Alice could be sensitive. "I'll wear it, but I won't be able to relax all night until it's safely off my head and back in its box."

Chef Heston strolled over, a large glass of red wine in his hand. "It looks like everyone's enjoying themselves. Are you having a good time, Holly?"

I nodded. This was the only time I ever saw Chef Heston relax.

"Of course, the food won't be as good as ours." He smiled at me.

"I believe the Duchess has hired a caterer from Harrods for this evening," Campbell said. "A member of my team was dispatched to collect him earlier when he got lost."

"Pah! Harrods has nothing on us," Chef Heston said. "Isn't that right, Holly? We're the best in the business."

"Yes, Chef," I said.

"Just for tonight, you may call me Quinton," Chef Heston said.

"I, um, thanks, Chef." There was no way I'd ever use his first name. I'd been calling him Chef ever since I started working here. As far as I was concerned, he didn't have a first name.

"Right, I'm off for a few rounds of gin rummy," Chef Heston said. "Have a fun night." He strolled away, laughing and chatting to people as he passed them.

"What game are you going to play tonight, Holly?" Campbell asked.

I was pretty certain there was a double meaning in those words. "I may start with a board game."

"I figured you were a murder mystery kind of girl. Didn't I see Clue set up in one corner?"

"I enjoy Clue, but the others don't like me to play."

"Because you always solve the murder before them?"

I shrugged. "I don't mean to. But sometimes, it's so obvious who did it."

"You would think that. Have a fun night," he said.

I did a quick circuit of the tables again, before settling on Monopoly. I'd just pulled up a chair, when someone dashed past the window. It was dark outside, so I couldn't see who it was, but they were moving fast.

I hopped from my seat and went to take a look.

The door to the saloon was shoved open. Betsy Malone stood there, gasping, her cheeks pink and her hair sticking up.

I hurried to her side. "Betsy, whatever's the matter?"

She placed a hand against her heaving chest. "There's a body outside. Somebody's been killed."

Chapter 15

After a few seconds of stunned silence, everyone in the room erupted in panic. They all talked at once as a crowd gathered around Betsy, trying to find out what was going on.

"Let me through." Campbell shoved past people until he reached Betsy. "Tell me what you saw. You said there's a body?"

Betsy drew in a shuddering breath. "I was just heading to games night from my cottage. I was running late, so I was hurrying. I saw a pile of rags on the lawn out the front. I almost didn't stop to look because I didn't want to miss the fun."

"Take your time," I said. I was worried Betsy might faint if she didn't get control of herself. Her breath kept shooting in and out in strangled little squeaks.

She glanced at me and nodded. "I hate seeing the grounds looking messy. They're always immaculate. I hurried over, thinking it was a tarp or sheet that had blown off a van. It wasn't until I got closer that I realized it was a person."

There were several gasps around us.

"Why do you think this person was killed?" Campbell asked.

"Because they have an arrow sticking out of their back," Betsy said.

Everyone in the room gasped again, and the muttering began. Several people moved toward the door.

"The body is out front?" Campbell asked.

Betsy nodded. "Halfway along the gravel driveway on the lawn. You can't miss it. He's wearing a white shirt."

"Everybody stay here," Campbell said. He strode away, already talking into his comms device.

"Do you know who it is?" I led Betsy to a chair, and she sat.

She gripped my hand and shook her head. "No. He was face down. I didn't recognize him from the back. I don't think it's anyone from the family, nor the staff. I know everyone here."

"Louise, can you take care of Betsy?" I looked over at Louise, who stood with Sally, both of them looking pale. "I need to go take a look at this."

"Of course," Louise said. "But do you really have to see the body? Isn't that a bit… gruesome?"

"We need to find out who it is," I said. "It could be someone we know."

"Don't get in trouble with Campbell by poking around," Betsy said. "He told everyone to stay here."

"And they're not listening." I nodded at the door. Several people were already creeping out.

"Be careful." Betsy squeezed my hand before Louise and Sally took over.

I hurried into the corridor and was met by Alice and Rupert.

"Is it true?" Alice said. "Someone else has been shot with an arrow?"

"Yes, but I don't know who it is," I said.

"Let's find out." Alice grabbed my hand.

Rupert hurried along beside us as we headed to the main doors. By the time we got outside, Campbell and half a dozen of his security team were on the lawn, gathered around what must be the body.

Several of the staff were lurking close by, trying to get a look.

I was about to wait with them, but Alice tugged me closer.

"Maybe we should give Campbell and his team a chance to work," I said.

"This is our house. I must know who's been killed on my front lawn," Alice said, not slowing as she approached the body. "Campbell, tell me what's going on."

His shoulders rose an inch as he turned. "Princess Alice, Lord Rupert. I must insist you return to the castle. There's been another shooting incident."

"We know that," Alice said. "That's why we're here. Who is it?"

I leaned past Campbell and took a peek at the body. "Is that Marcel?"

Campbell's gaze narrowed before he nodded. "That's right."

"But... he's our prime suspect in Ben's murder," I said.

"Not anymore," Campbell said. "Please, return to the safety of the castle. There could be evidence that's being contaminated by everyone being out here."

"Good idea. Let's move back," Rupert said.

"I appreciate that, Lord Rupert," Campbell said.

"From the way Marcel is lying, maybe he didn't see the arrow coming," I said, my gaze glued to the body.

"Or he was running away from whoever was shooting at him," Alice said. "How many arrows have you found, Campbell?"

Campbell huffed out a breath. "So far, just the one in the victim's back."

"What was he doing out here on his own?" I asked.

"We'll find out what he was doing soon enough," Campbell said. "But only if you let me do my job."

I backed up a few steps, but Alice refused to move as she stared at the body.

"Whoever shot him must be an excellent archer," she said. "Do you see, the arrow is dead center in his back? That shot wasn't a fluke. Someone skilled with a bow killed Marcel."

"Well observed, Princess." Campbell gestured at the castle before flashing me a look of desperation.

I was trying to get Alice to move, but she could be as stubborn as Meatball when he found a giant stick he wanted to carry.

Alice lifted a hand and smiled. "Just to let everybody know, it wasn't me. I'm the best shooter around here, but I was in the kitchen with Rupert, sorting out the food for games night. The Duchess was there as well."

"Thank you for offering an alibi, Princess Alice. I'm certain you had nothing to do with this," Campbell said.

"What's going on out here?" Johann, Penny, and Evelyn appeared on the edge of the lawn.

"That's just what we're trying to find out," Campbell muttered.

I glanced over at them and stepped closer to Campbell. "Those are the potential suspects for this murder. They all knew Marcel. Perhaps they had something to do with this."

Campbell gestured at two of his men, and they hurried over. "Clear this area. The crime scene evidence will be worthless if we're not careful."

"What about the suspects?" I gestured to the crowd.

He shook his head and turned away. I'd been dismissed once again.

Campbell's team launched into action, and we were pushed to the edge of the lawn with everyone else, much to Alice's annoyance.

"We should be right there," she said. "We can help Campbell figure this out."

"He doesn't want us involved. He's made that clear." I watched Campbell at work, itching to get involved but knowing I'd only get yelled at or snubbed. "That was a good spot with the arrow."

Alice shrugged. "That was obvious. Anyone who knows one end of a longbow from the other could have seen that the shooter has skills."

"That print is no good to us now," Kace said to Campbell as they walked toward us.

I hurried toward them, Alice right by my side. "What print are you talking about?"

Campbell shot a furious glare at Kace, who lifted a hand before backing off. "Sorry, boss."

"Did you find something on the body?" I asked. "A clue to the shooter?"

Campbell let out a sigh. "I suppose you'll find out anyway, given your incessant snooping."

"I'm not an incessant snooper. I'm—"

"Hush, or I won't tell you anything."

I mimed zipping my lips shut, and Alice giggled.

Campbell nodded. "I was looking closely at Marcel as Ben's killer. The print Kace was referring to relates to a partial fingerprint found on an arrow in the woods. It was a match for Marcel."

"Did you question him about it?"

"No, and I won't get the chance to now. This second murder shows our killer is still out there. The print is worthless."

I tapped my finger against my chin. "Unless Marcel killed Ben, then someone killed Marcel to get revenge for what happened." I looked at Penny. A grief-stricken girlfriend was an obvious suspect, but she didn't know how to shoot.

"Stop right there with your theories," Campbell said. "We have a dangerous, unstable individual who's skilled with a bow and arrow on the loose. Until they're caught, everyone must proceed with extreme caution. This isn't a safe place. I'll be instructing the family to leave the castle until this is solved."

"No! I'm not going anywhere," Alice said. "I refuse to be driven out of my home by a criminal."

"Princess Alice, it's for your own good. I'm recommending to the Duchess that you leave by the end of the evening."

"And I'll be recommending to her that—"

"We should listen to Campbell," Rupert said as he approached. "It is his job to protect us. And he's right. Someone in this crowd could be the killer."

"If anyone shoots an arrow at me, I'll shoot one right back," Alice said. "I'm not leaving."

"Holly, a word in private," Campbell said.

Before I had a chance to respond, he yanked me out of earshot of Alice and Rupert.

"Please get Princess Alice to see sense," he said. "She listens to you. I can't have her life put at risk because she's being stubborn. She's vulnerable. The whole family is."

"You know Alice, she digs in her heels when she doesn't agree about something. If you can't convince her to leave, I won't have any chance of doing so."

He looked at the crowd of onlookers before sighing. "Then we have to find the killer and find them fast."

I pressed my lips together to stop a smile from blossoming. "Does that mean you need my help?"

He grunted. "It's going to be all hands on deck to solve this double murder."

"That wasn't an answer. If you need my insight into this case, you only have to ask. Of course, I could always side with Princess Alice. Maybe there is no danger here and we should stay put."

He growled low in his chest. "You're pushing your luck, Holmes."

I lifted my hands. "I've spoken to everyone who could be involved with these murders. I know the suspects as well as you do. Maybe together, we can figure this out and make sure the family stay safe. I definitely don't want them to be at risk."

"We're all at risk while we're outside," Campbell said. "For all I know, the shooter could be on the castle turret lining up another strike."

I swallowed, my gaze flashing skyward. "You have your guys checking that out, right?"

He smirked. "Naturally."

"Then how about we get everyone inside? Your team do their job, and I'll speak to Princess Alice. At the very least, I'll get her to stay inside the castle until we figure out what happened to Marcel."

He scraped a hand down his face. "I guess that's the best we can do."

I looked over to where Johann, Penny, and Evelyn stood. "We'll find out who did this. This is all linked to history, I just know it. My gut is never wrong."

"Your gut is no use to me. We need evidence," Campbell said.

"Then let me help you find it." I stuck out my hand. "Shall we be partners?"

He scowled before giving my hand a brisk shake. "Agreed. You deal with the Princess, I'll sort out the body."

I grinned. "It'll be my pleasure, partner."

Chapter 16

It had been a struggle, but I'd managed to get Alice and Rupert back inside the castle without any incident. And, after a long conversation with her, she'd agreed to stay inside until the killer had been found.

It had gone midnight before everyone finally went to bed; me included. But I'd had a restless night, thinking about Marcel's murder and who shot that arrow at him.

I rolled over and blinked my tired eyes at the clock by the side of my bed. It wasn't yet six in the morning, and I felt like I'd only had a couple of hours sleep. I yawned and stretched.

Meatball bounced onto my bed, a squeaky toy in his mouth.

"Good morning, handsome." I gave him a cuddle and a belly rub. "We need to figure this out. Who's going around shooting people?"

Meatball jumped off the bed, giving a gentle woof as he hit the floor. He returned with a chewy rubber bone in his mouth, which he dropped by my feet.

"Thank you." I tossed the bone in the air, and he grabbed it. "Ben and Marcel's murders must be linked.

They were both assistants to Professor Stephen, that's one thing they had in common."

"Woof, woof." Meatball discarded the bone and bounced off the bed again, returning with a small, chewed tennis ball.

I scratched behind his ears. "They were also competing for the same grant money. Could there be a rival for that money I don't know about? Someone who killed Marcel and Ben to get their hands on the grant?"

"Woof." Meatball didn't seem impressed by that idea. He disappeared again and returned with a googly eyed teddy bear that was missing an ear.

"You're right, that seems a bit of a stretch," I said. "It would look suspicious if the people in line for the grant money started dying. The police would easily pick up that link, as would Campbell. Plus, this mystery person would have needed to know that Ben and Marcel were here, and have the skills to slip past castle security. We should scratch that idea. It's someone already here. Someone we've met."

"Woof, woof." Meatball bounced off the bed again. This time, he returned with his empty food bowl, which he placed carefully on my knees, a hopeful glint in his eyes.

"Okay, hint taken. You're hungry. So am I. I didn't have dinner last night. We missed out on the games night food thanks to the not so small problem of a murder."

Meatball placed a paw over his nose.

"I agree, it's a tragedy. We can make up for it by having a big, delicious breakfast." I climbed out of bed, put on my robe and slippers, and let Meatball out to do his morning business, before making us both breakfast. He had kibble and a scoop of his favorite wet premium dog food, and I made pancakes.

I settled at the table and dug my fork into my maple syrup covered pancakes. "Maybe Ben and Marcel knew something about Professor Stephen. Something he didn't want anyone else to know. They'd have had access to his files, maybe even his journals or a private diary if he keeps one."

Meatball didn't lift his nose from his bowl but wagged his tail to show he was listening.

"They could have learned something bad about him, and he needed to ensure their silence, so he shot them." I ate another piece of pancake. "But what about his back injury? And his alibi for Ben's murder. We'll have to see where he was when Marcel was shot."

A muffled woof came from Meatball's bowl.

"And then there's Johann. His lucky arrow story could have been a cover, and he did kill Ben during the shooting contest. Maybe he got worried Marcel had seen him. They were collecting arrows together that day. He shot him to make sure he didn't tell anyone."

That earned me another wag of Meatball's tail. So far, I was no closer to discovering who had killed Ben and Marcel. I was certain the two murders were linked. I just needed to figure out what that link was.

"Let's stick with Professor Stephen for now," I said. "Ben and Marcel worked for him, which is a direct association. The next step is to figure out how to get access to Professor Stephen and make him talk. When he was relaxed during his massage, he was quick to get chatty."

Meatball trotted away from his empty bowl and over to the table. He hopped up and waggled his front paws at me in the hope of getting a piece of pancake.

"You look like a hula dancer," I said. "All you need is a garland of flowers around your neck and—" My eyes widened. "Of course. Alice's hula chair."

"Woof, woof?" Meatball dropped down and cocked his head.

"Let's use the hula chair on Professor Stephen. We could say it'll help his back pain. A gentle, rotating massage could be just what he needs."

Meatball sneezed before shaking his head.

"I think it's a great idea. It's worth a go," I said. "Let's see if Alice is up for it." I grabbed my phone and sent her a message.

Got a plan to get Professor Stephen to talk. Need your help. Are you free?

I'd just eaten the next bite of my pancake before a message pinged on my phone.

Of course. How are we going to do that?

You need to invite him for a session on the hula chair.

The response I got back was a long string of question marks.

Meet you in your room in half an hour.

She replied with a big smiley face.

I finished my breakfast, grabbed a quick shower, and dressed so I was ready for work. I had an hour before I needed to get baking. That should give me just enough time to put this plan into action.

"Sorry, Meatball. Just a short walk this morning, but I'll make it up to you later."

He didn't seem to mind and was happy to leave the apartment as I hurried to the castle to meet Alice. We did ten minutes around the lawn before I tucked him in his kennel by the kitchen with a big, meaty-smelling chew strip.

I hurried through the main door of the castle and up the stairs to Alice's room. I knocked on the door, and she pulled it open straight away.

She grabbed my arm and pulled me inside before shutting the door. "What's my hula chair got to do with getting a confession out of Professor Stephen?"

"I'm not sure I'm looking for a confession," I said. "But he may know the connection between Ben and Marcel and why they were killed."

"Okay, but what's my chair got to do with it?"

"Professor Stephen has a bad back. I figured a session on the chair would loosen up his muscles and give us a chance to question him. But you need to sell it to him. He doesn't know me. I'm sure if he gets an invitation from a princess, he won't be able to refuse."

"Oh! That's genius, and also very true. I am rather fabulous. Everyone wants to spend time with me." She clapped her hands together. "I'll have my chair taken to the crimson room. Hardly anyone is allowed in there, so it'll be extra special for him. And I know Professor Stephen and Evelyn haven't gone to breakfast yet. I saw her in the corridor ten minutes ago. We can grab them before they go down."

"Good idea. It's probably best not to use the hula chair on a full stomach, anyway."

"And I'll say you're there as my lady's maid. Professor Stephen won't think it's odd if you're lurking around in the background."

"Perfect. Although Evelyn knows I work in the kitchen. She may think it's a bit odd."

"I'll explain it away if she questions things. She won't think I'm lying. And I have the option to send her to the dungeon if she gets too nosy. Give me five minutes to organize the chair being moved," Alice said. "You keep an eye out for Professor Stephen and make sure he doesn't go down for breakfast. You'll see them as they come down the stairs."

I hurried out of her room and loitered around the corridor, keeping a lookout for either Professor Stephen or Evelyn descending from the second-floor guest wing.

Alice came out of her room a few minutes later, just as two members of Campbell's security team appeared.

"Right this way," she said to them. "The chair needs to go to the crimson room immediately."

They got to work, and the chair swiftly vanished along the corridor.

"Couldn't you have gotten someone else to move the chair?" I asked. "Campbell will hear about this if we're not careful. He wants to keep you out of danger."

"Don't worry about him. And it would have taken too long to get anyone else. They don't mind helping. Plus, they have the muscles to do it. Those chairs are heavy."

I smiled and shook my head. They had no choice but to help when Princess Alice clicked her fingers.

"Any sign of our target?" Alice asked.

"Not yet," I said.

"Then what are we waiting for? He can't still be in bed. And if he is, it's time he got up." Alice grabbed my arm and pulled me along the corridor and up the stairs to the guest wing. She knocked on Professor Stephen's door.

Evelyn opened it a few seconds later. "Princess Alice. It's nice to see you again."

"And you," she said. "I've been so worried about your husband. How is he this morning?"

Evelyn glanced over her shoulder and stepped closer. "Still not good. And what with the stress of Marcel dying yesterday, it's not helping his healing. I wonder whether it's better if we just leave."

"I don't think anyone can leave at the moment," Alice said. "The castle security team still need to talk to everyone again and figure out what happened."

She shook her head. "I suppose so. It's terribly sad. And Stephen has lost his appetite. It's all the stress. And he also had a strange experience when he had his massage yesterday. I don't think that helped with his recovery."

I bit my lip and looked away.

"I have the perfect solution for all of that," Alice said. "May I come in for a moment and speak to your husband?"

"Of course," Evelyn said. She nodded at me as we entered the room. "Darling, Princess Alice and her friend are here to see you."

Professor Stephen hobbled out of the attached bathroom. "Good morning, Princess." His gaze went to me, but there was no recognition in his eyes.

"I have something to help with your bad back," Alice said. "It's a revolutionary new massage chair. It gently stimulates the muscles whilst aiding healing."

Professor Stephen let out a sigh, and his hand went to his lower back. "That's what I need. The massage I had the other day helped a little, but I still feel tender. Where do I need to go to try this chair?"

"I own one," Alice said. "I've had it set up in the crimson room downstairs."

His eyes widened. "The crimson room! That room has barely been touched since it was created in the seventeen hundreds. I believe there are numerous paintings of the house and grounds to explore in that room. How exciting. What a treat."

"I thought you'd enjoy being in there," Alice said. "I hope it makes up for you being injured during the shooting."

"It absolutely does. Thank you so much, Princess."

"My pleasure," Alice said. "And you must try the chair before breakfast. It's wonderful. I always use it to help with muscle fatigue and discomfort."

"It's a very generous gesture," Evelyn said. "How exciting, darling."

"I always make sure my guests are well looked after. Why don't we go right now?" Alice said.

"I could do with a cup of coffee before I get moving," Professor Stephen said.

"Holly, you get the refreshments. I'll take my guests to the crimson room." She stepped closer. "I won't start any interrogation until you get there."

"Of course, Princess." I hurried to the kitchen and dashed around getting together coffee for everyone.

"You're here early." Chef Heston strode into the kitchen, an espresso cup in his hand.

"I'm getting refreshments for Princess Alice and her guests."

"Are you now? Don't be late getting here today. And don't think I didn't notice you vanish the other afternoon. You owe me some time."

"Um, what afternoon are you talking about?" I kept my back to him as I poured hot water into the cafetière.

"You know which afternoon."

I gulped. Chef Heston missed nothing when it came to his kitchen. "It won't happen again, Chef. And I won't be late for my shift this morning." I grabbed the tray and hurried out before he kept questioning me.

I dashed to the crimson room, arriving just as Professor Stephen, Evelyn, and Alice entered.

"Perfect timing, Holly." Alice winked at me.

I nodded and set down the tray.

"This is what I was telling you about, Professor Stephen." Alice gestured around the room. "Everything is set out just as my ancestors wished. Nothing has changed in hundreds of years."

I looked around, fascinated to be in this mysterious part of the castle. I'd never been in the room. It was something of a mystery, a time capsule into the past.

My initial excitement faded. The dark wooden furniture and deep red dressings made it feel small and claustrophobic.

"What a charming room," Evelyn said. "Are the artworks all original?"

"Of course," Alice said. "My ancestor filled this room with his favorites. He'd sit in here for ages and study them."

"Extraordinary," Professor Stephen said. His gaze settled on the chair, his forehead wrinkling. "You're sure this chair is safe to use?"

"Very safe," Alice said. "And excellent for bad backs. Hop on and give it a try."

"It looks like it could be fun." Evelyn walked around the chair. "I wouldn't mind having a go myself."

"You absolutely can," Alice said. "Let's help your husband's back first."

"I need a sip of coffee before we begin," Professor Stephen said.

I hurried over with a mug, which he took with a grateful nod, and took a sip.

I passed around coffee for everyone, before moving to stand beside Alice.

After Professor Stephen had drunk his coffee, he handed his mug to his wife and settled in the chair. "What do I do now?"

"Hold on to the arm rests and make sure you're comfortable." Alice knelt beside the chair. "All I do is press this button. It has variable speeds, so once you're used to the motion, you can go faster to see if it helps your back."

"I'm willing to try anything if it makes me feel better." Professor Stephen gripped the arms of the chair.

"Are you ready?" Alice asked.

"Let's do this," he said.

Alice smiled up at him before pressing the button.

"Goodness!" His knuckles went white as he clung to the chair arm. "I didn't expect it to rotate like this. What an odd feeling."

"It's excellent for your core." Alice backed away from the chair. She stood beside me and leaned over until her mouth was by my ear. "We didn't plan what questions I need to ask."

"Talk about Marcel," I whispered under the hum of the hula chair.

"How does that feel, darling?" Evelyn asked.

"It's most strange," Professor Stephen said. "I'm not sure it's helping. My back is tingling."

"That's good. Give it a few minutes to get everything loosened up," Alice said. "You'll feel so much better after a session on the chair."

The look on his face suggested he felt anything but comfortable.

Alice cleared her throat. "I'm so sorry about what happened to your assistant. Not Ben, although that's sad too, but Marcel."

Professor Stephen shook his head. "We heard the commotion outside, and Evelyn went to take a look. I was stunned when she returned and told me what was going on."

"Would you like to go faster?" Alice asked. She hit the button to speed up the chair before he answered. The hula chair groaned and rocked faster.

Professor Stephen clutched the arms. "I'm feeling queasy. I don't think I can last much longer."

"Breathe through your nose and you'll be fine," Alice said. "Did you have a good relationship with Marcel? I expect you'll find it hard to replace him."

"I suppose I will. He'd been a student at the university for three years," Professor Stephen said. "I can't understand why anyone would want him dead. I was thinking of making him my prime assistant. With Ben gone, Marcel would have had a chance at doing some decent research."

Evelyn rested a hand on his shoulder. "Two smart young men gone too soon. It's a loss to the university."

He patted her hand. "I'll continue their work. They both had solid research projects they were working on. I'll get those published. It's the least I can do for them. It'll be something to remember them by."

"You could write a book based on their work," Evelyn said. "Didn't you mention Ben had a good idea for a project?"

"That won't be possible. I've already got a hectic work schedule for the next year. Maybe in the future."

"You could dedicate the books to them," Evelyn said. "That would be a fitting way to give them a lasting legacy."

"I'll give it some thought. They were good students. I'd like to do something to remember them."

"I could always arrange a fundraiser," Evelyn said.

"A fundraiser?" Alice said.

"Oh, yes. It's what I focus on. I'm always organizing gatherings to raise money so Stephen can complete his work. The last event we held was at Norwich Castle. It was a gateway to medieval England, and such a fascinating place that it drew quite a crowd of notable historians. We raised a good sum of money."

"That would be a generous way of remembering Marcel and Ben," Alice said. "You could use the money for a memorial."

"Like a garden bench?" Professor Stephen said.

"Darling, I think we can raise a little more money than that." Evelyn patted his shoulder.

"I'll be sure to contribute," Alice said. "I can't help but feel a tiny bit guilty, since their deaths happened on our grounds. People will stop coming to the castle if this keeps happening."

"You shouldn't worry about that," Professor Stephen said. "Audley Castle is a magnificent historical monument. I expect murders only add to people's interest in the place."

"I hadn't considered that," Alice said. "It's a gruesome thought. People actually want to visit murder sites?"

"It's a popular hobby for some," Professor Stephen said. "People pay money to wander around London looking at the locations where Jack the Ripper slayed his victims."

Alice was silent for a moment before striding over and hitting the speed button. The hula chair groaned in response and whizzed around faster. "How do you feel now?"

"Still queasy, and my back's not doing too well," Professor Stephen said. "Maybe we can stop in a minute and look at the paintings."

"We're almost done." Alice walked back to me, her wide eyes suggesting she was panicking. "What do I ask now?"

"Has he been questioned about his alibi last night?" I muttered out of the side of my mouth.

She turned and faced Professor Stephen. "I hope my security team hasn't been too invasive with questions about Marcel. They are very thorough, and they do need to find out what happened to him."

"They've not been a problem," Professor Stephen said. "They came to see us last night and asked a few questions about where we were. They were satisfied when they learned we were in our room."

"You didn't leave the whole evening?" Alice asked. "I don't want you getting bored and feel you're trapped in that room. I could arrange for some entertainment if you'd like."

"That's very kind of you," Evelyn said. "But our entertainment needs are simple. My husband is either researching, working, or reading."

"Or sleeping," he said. "The doctor gave me some strong pain medication to take the edge off my back. The pills help, but I get so tired."

"And I'm happy to entertain myself with my books. I also do needlework. We're fine as we are. Please, don't worry about us."

"Is there any chance you can stop this chair?" Professor Stephen had gone a pale shade of green.

"Only if you're feeling better," Alice said.

"Oh! Yes, so much better. I feel like a new man."

Alice glanced at me, and I nodded. It didn't look like we'd get any more useful information out of Professor Stephen. And if we kept torturing him on the hula chair, he may just vomit.

Alice hurried over and stopped the chair. Professor Stephen and the hula chair both groaned.

He clutched his wife's arm as he staggered to his feet. "If you'll excuse us, Princess, we're going to head down to breakfast now. Although I may need to go back to the room for a few minutes to recover from this experience."

"Of course. Enjoy the rest of your day," Alice said.

Professor Stephen limped away, aided by Evelyn, who had her arm hooked around his waist.

"What do you think about Professor Stephen? Did he kill Marcel?" Alice asked. "He didn't come over as nervous about anything."

"He can't be the killer. He has an alibi, and his back is still troubling him."

"I agree. I don't think it was him," Alice said. "He talked about leaving a legacy for Ben and Marcel. He wouldn't want a legacy of his crimes anywhere near him. It would be a reminder of his guilt."

I nodded. "He's off the hook. Which leaves us with Johann. I'd discounted him from Ben's murder, but he's a man at the end of his tether, and that can make a person act irrationally. Do you know if Campbell or the police have spoken to him about what happened to Marcel?"

"Not as far as I know," Alice said. "I can check. I'll summon Campbell for an update."

"Let's not summon Campbell. It'll only make him angry when he learns what we're up to. Johann appeared after Marcel's body was discovered," I said.

"Along with Penny and Evelyn," Alice said.

"Maybe he killed Marcel, then raced down from the turret. He could have turned up with them to make it look like he was innocent. We have to check his alibi."

"And if it was Johann, we have to figure out how to get him to confess," Alice said.

"Without proof he's the shooter, that won't be easy."

"It may not be easy, but Johann does like a drink. We can exploit that," Alice said. "We get him drunk and make him talk."

"It won't do any harm to try to loosen his tongue," I said. "He was willing enough to talk to me when I found him in the woods looking for his arrow. But I doubt we'll get a confession out of him. If he's behind these murders, he's not going to let that slip out, no matter how sozzled he gets."

"One step at a time," Alice said, a big smile on her face. "Let's get drunk and see what happens."

Chapter 17

The rest of the morning and most of the afternoon passed in a blur of frantic baking. The plan to get Johann to talk was well underway, all thanks to Alice and her powers of persuasion.

Chef Heston stomped into the kitchen from the main hallway. "Is everything ready?"

I looked up, a piping bag posed over the cakes in front of me. "Almost. I'm just finishing icing the mini espresso martini cakes. The drunken chocolate truffle cake, brandy infused Madeira cake, and the mini Irish coffee cakes are all done."

He shook his head and pursed his lips. "I wish Princess Alice had given us more notice. Doesn't she know we have a busy café to run? She simply dropped the request for a special afternoon tea and expected me to fit her in."

"I don't mind adding these cakes to my normal baking schedule." Even though I hadn't stopped for so much as a cup of tea since I started, finding the killer was the most important thing.

He grunted. "So long as you don't let the rest of your baking get behind. We're getting low on cherry cream pies in the café."

I pointed to the chiller where a dozen pies sat. "They're all ready to go. I'd never let our visitors go hungry."

He walked over and stared into the chiller. "Very well. This is so inconvenient. Why does Princess Alice want you to serve the food for this party?"

I focused on swirling the icing over the cakes. "The Princess is exacting when it comes to her parties. She likes everything to be just so. I won't be long. It won't affect my work."

He lifted his chin. "You need to be careful, Holly."

I lowered my icing bag, my stomach doing a flip. Did he know what we were planning? "Careful of what?"

"Princess Alice treats you like her favorite pet poodle," he said. "And you run around after her all the time."

"I don't. I'm not her pet poodle," I said, indignation making my insides warm. "We're friends."

"Kitchen staff and princesses can't be friends," Chef Heston said. "We're here to serve the family."

I frowned at him. "I understand that. But Princess Alice likes me."

"Until you put a foot wrong," he said. "We aren't meant to associate with the upper class. Besides, what's the problem with working in a kitchen and having friends here?"

"There's no problem, and I have friends here," I said. "I can't be friends with Princess Alice as well?"

He lifted a hand. "I've seen this sort of thing before. It didn't end well."

"How did it end?"

"With someone losing their job. And it wasn't a member of the family."

My brows lowered. "Princess Alice would never treat anyone so badly."

"Don't say I didn't warn you. If it's not Princess Alice issuing orders for you to serve her, Lady Philippa wants you to take her cake. If you get tangled up in this family, you could get in trouble."

"Yes, Chef." I refused to look at him and stabbed my piping nozzle at the cakes.

He huffed at me before walking away.

I couldn't agree with him. I was good friends with Alice. And she'd been the one to initiate our friendship. I understood it was strange that I was such good friends with members of the family, but that wasn't something I could help. Chef Heston was wrong. I was helping out a friend. And she was helping me, too.

Alice had planned an exclusive boozy afternoon tea for the remaining members of the history party. There'd be champagne cocktails, Sunset Rum punch, and Remy Martin brandy, not to mention all the booze-soaked cakes I'd spent hours preparing today. If this didn't get Johann drunk and talking, nothing would.

I finished my icing and loaded the trolley with the delicious treats before heading out of the kitchen and over to the drawing room.

I was setting everything out on a long table covered in a white linen cloth when Campbell strode in.

"What are you up to?"

I turned and gave him a sweet smile. "Organizing Princess Alice's afternoon gathering."

"I heard there was a last-minute change to the schedule." He walked over and looked down at the cakes. "What a coincidence that all the remaining suspects in the murder investigations have been invited."

I turned away and lined up the champagne glasses. "Isn't it? I was just thinking that."

"You're not fooling me," he said. "You're behind this."

I finished with the glasses and turned to face him. "This is simply a generous gesture of Princess Alice's. After everything they've gone through, she wanted to give the remaining guests something pleasant to focus on. Don't you think they need it?"

"They do. What they don't need is you poking around and asking them intrusive questions."

"My questions are never intrusive," I said. "They're helpful and insightful, as all good partner's questions should be. Unless you've changed your mind about me helping you to figure this out, I don't see the problem."

His nostrils expanded. "I haven't. Especially since the Duke and Duchess sided with Princess Alice. The family has refused to leave the castle."

"So, you can't object to this. We could be about to uncover the killer."

"It's a big risk you're taking, especially because you've involved Princess Alice again."

I tutted and straightened the napkins. "That's her choice. Princess Alice is a modern, independent woman with a mind of her own."

"She's stubborn. And you make her worse."

"I encourage independence, there's nothing wrong with that. Now, if I ask you a question about the progress you're making with Marcel's murder investigation, will you answer it, partner?"

"I'll answer your questions, if you answer mine."

"Good enough. Who have you got as a prime suspect for Marcel's shooting?"

"There aren't many people left to choose from," he said.

"That's exactly what I've been thinking," I said. "And I've ruled out Professor Stephen."

"Explain your reasoning behind that."

"He's still injured. I confirmed that this morning."

"Did you venture into his room and give him another rubdown?"

My cheeks grew warm. "No! That was... an unfortunate event. But I couldn't let an opportunity go by to question a suspect when he was off guard."

Campbell arched an eyebrow. "Is there anything you wouldn't do to catch a killer?"

"I probably wouldn't shoot someone if they made a run for it." I tilted my head, my gaze going to Campbell's sidearm. "Have you ever shot anyone?"

He raised his gaze to the ceiling. "Despite what you say, I'm still interested in Professor Stephen."

"Then you're wasting your time. He was with Evelyn when both murders took place. And when Marcel was killed, they were in their bedroom."

Campbell nodded. "That's the alibi we got as well."

"You don't believe him?"

"Sometimes, a wife will cover for her husband if she loves him enough, or if he terrifies her enough that she'll say anything he tells her to."

"Evelyn isn't scared of Professor Stephen. They're fond of each other. She's been taking care of him since he got injured."

"Do you think she loves him enough to lie for him?"

I twisted a napkin in my hands. "I'm not certain. But Professor Stephen is genuinely hurt, and Evelyn can't shoot. They're in the clear. Which leaves us with Johann."

"Ah, I get it." He waved a hand in the air. "You're planning on interrogating Johann over fruit cake and champagne."

"Booze infused cake and lashings of potent alcohol," I said. "And it'll be a very gentle interrogation we conduct. Alcohol is his weakness."

"The *we* meaning you and Princess Alice?"

"They'd hardly come to a party arranged by the kitchen assistant," I said.

"And if I tell you not to do this because it's reckless and puts Princess Alice at risk?" Campbell asked.

"Then you'd be going against her direct wishes, and you know what she threatens to do to people who disobey her."

Campbell sighed and looked around the room. "I can position some men close by. We'll keep an eye on the situation and make sure you don't lose control."

"It's going to be a genteel afternoon party. It's not as if a fight will break out, or the killer will come armed with his longbow." I chewed on my bottom lip.

"From your ominous silence, you must be realizing the flaws in your plan."

I scowled at Campbell. "There aren't any flaws. The one problem I have is that I'm not convinced Johann's the killer, but he's the only one left that I haven't discounted. We need to get to the bottom of this mystery."

"What you need to do is tread carefully. If Johann fired those arrows, you could spook him. He'll make a run for it before we arrest him. We need concrete evidence that he killed Ben and Marcel. Right now, there's no physical evidence or motive for him wanting either of them dead."

"Which is why this party is the perfect way to get some proof," I said. "We were both leaning toward Marcel as Ben's killer, but these deaths have to be linked. We need to find out if there's a connection between Ben, Marcel, and Johann. Once we know that, we can discover the motive for him wanting them dead."

"I'm still not happy about this," Campbell said.

"You can't cancel the party," I said. "And you need to leave. Johann has been invited to arrive half an hour earlier than everyone else so we can get him on his own and question him."

Campbell didn't move, despite me making shooing gestures at him. "You're planning on interrogating a potential double murderer on your own?"

"Holly won't be on her own." Alice swept into the room, looking resplendent in a cream silk dress that skimmed her knees. "I'll be by her side. And I'm leading on the questioning. Nobody would dare lay a finger on me. If they did, they know I'd set you on them. You always look after me." She fluttered her lashes at Campbell.

"I'll be watching your every move, Princess." Campbell took a step back, the tips of his ears growing pink.

"I can always rely on you," Alice said. Her gaze ran over the food. "This is perfect. Now, all we need is for our suspect to arrive, and we can get this interrogation started."

Campbell glared at me. I was getting good at reading those glares. This one looked like it said *if you do anything to put Princess Alice in harm's way, I will hunt you down and destroy you.*

"That'll be all, Campbell." Alice nodded at him.

"Of course." He gave me one more glare before leaving the room.

"I hope he wasn't telling you off," Alice said.

"He was warning me," I said. "And he'd be right to do so. We need to be careful around Johann. Maybe his drunken bumbling is just an act."

"We're about to find out," Alice said. "I saw him heading out of his room a couple of minutes ago. He'll be here soon. You pour the champagne cocktails, and I'll be ready to pounce the second he arrives."

I got to work on the drinks, just as Johann walked into the room.

He looked around. "Am I early? I can come back if you're not ready for guests."

Alice hurried over and grasped his arm. "No, you're right on time. Don't worry about everyone else, they'll be here soon. While we wait, what can I get you to drink?"

Johann's eyes lit up as he saw the drink laden table. "I wouldn't mind a large brandy."

"Holly, prepare Johann his drink." Alice pointed out the food. "It's a boozy party, so everything is laced with alcohol."

"That sounds right up my street." Johann accepted his brandy from me and took a large slug.

Alice kept hold of his elbow. "How are you feeling after what happened to Marcel?"

His shoulders slumped, and his gaze lowered. "I'm in shock."

"I saw you outside not long after it happened. Where were you when you heard the news?" Alice asked.

"I was wandering around the gallery with Penny. We were looking at the artwork, when we heard people yelling. We followed the noise and came outside." He shook his head. "Who would do such a thing?"

"My security team is figuring that out," Alice said. "First Ben and now Marcel. Do you think the murders are connected?"

"I haven't really thought about it." Johann drank more of his brandy. "I suppose it makes sense. They were killed in the same way."

"And they were students at the same university, isn't that right?" Alice said. "Do you think that could be the connection?"

"Goodness. You have given this some consideration," Johann said.

"I'm more interested in your thoughts," Alice said. "Was the work they were doing risky or unpopular?"

"No! They studied history," Johann said. "That's not something you kill over. They were researchers, nothing more. Stephen will be gutted they're both dead. He'll need to find more pawns." He downed his brandy.

Alice grabbed the empty glass and gave it to me to refill. "What do you mean by pawns?"

I let out a sigh of relief, glad she'd picked up on that strange comment. Alice was getting good at questioning suspects.

"Ah, I shouldn't have said anything." Johann drank more brandy and helped himself to a piece of Madeira cake. "Are these artworks on the walls originals?"

"Of course," Alice said. She glanced at me, and I nodded at her to continue her questioning. "Were Ben and Marcel into art history?"

He gazed at a painting for several seconds. "No, they were into the British Tudor period. Although Marcel liked the Dark Ages as well. And Ben was focused on a new find discovered during the excavation of a medieval monastery."

"Princess Alice, if I may?" I hadn't planned on interrupting, but the way Johann described Ben and Marcel as pawns had made a connection in my head. Was he somehow using their talents to further his own career?

"Of course." Alice nodded at me. "Holly is a friend of mine, Johann. You don't object if she asks you a question?"

Johann shrugged. "Fine by me. Holly helped me out of a difficult situation, so I'm in her debt."

"Thanks. Professor Stephen suggested he would publish Ben and Marcel's unfinished work," I said. "It's a nice way to remember them, don't you think?"

Johann shook his head and snorted a laugh. "I bet he can't wait to do that. He'd have published it anyway, even if they were alive. And he had a particular interest in Ben's thesis."

"You've lost me," Alice said, her gaze shifting from Johann to me.

Johann gulped down more brandy. He grabbed another cake and took a bite. "This is delicious. It tastes just like an Irish liqueur." He ate two pieces before finishing his second large glass of brandy and hiccupping.

I nodded at Alice. She needed to keep the questions rolling.

Confusion flashed across her face, and she shrugged at me.

"Tell us more about what Professor Stephen would do with Ben's work," I said. "It sounds interesting." It also sounded like he had something to gain.

Johann shrugged. "It's not that interesting, but it is immoral. Stephen's an ideas thief. He picks the brightest students and takes them on to mentor. He encourages them to produce ground-breaking work. These students, who have yet to make a name for themselves, have the luxury of creating all kinds of new theories. They get to run with them because they have nothing to lose by proposing something unique. It's clever of him to use them in that way."

"What does Professor Stephen do with those ideas?" Alice asked. "You called him an ideas thief. I'm not sure what that means."

"I think I do." I'd always considered it incredible how Professor Stephen had so many diverse theories. He could jump from revolutionary ideas about agriculture, to proposing a radical new concept on royal rule and privilege without breaking a sweat. Normally, that kind of work would take years to research and refine.

"His brilliant ideas are stolen from other people," I said.

Johann glanced at me. He passed over his empty brandy glass, and I refilled it and handed it back. "That's it in a nutshell. He uses his students to complete the research and ensure the idea is tangible, then he claims it as his own and publishes a paper."

"That doesn't sound right," Alice said. "What do his students think about that?"

"It doesn't matter what they think. He's the one people pay attention to. If any student claims his work was stolen, he wouldn't be taken seriously. After all, they worked under the great Professor Stephen Maguire. Everyone would take his side. Everyone would also think it was the student who'd stolen the project and was attempting to make a name for themselves."

"I've read all of Professor Stephen's books," I said. "None of it was his work?"

"Johann. You need to be careful about spreading rumors like that. With your lousy reputation, people could think you're not being honest."

We all turned to the door. Professor Stephen stood there, his narrowed gaze fixed on Johann.

"Oh! I didn't realize you'd arrived." Johann spilled brandy over the side of his glass. He took several steps toward Professor Stephen before coming to a halt and looking back at us.

"Do you have any proof of those accusations?" Professor Stephen strode into the room.

"I didn't mean to say anything." Johann looked at the glass in his hand. "I don't know what came over me."

"Several large brandies by the looks of it," Professor Stephen said. He turned to Princess Alice and bowed. "Take no notice of him. Johann is a washed up drunk who's about to lose his job. He's desperate for attention and is clearly on the road to ruin."

"Stephen! We're friends." Johann placed his glass down and adjusted his shirt cuffs. "How can you say such things?"

"We used to be friends," Professor Stephen said. "After the insidious lies I just heard coming out of your mouth, we can no longer be considered friendly. And, as we both know, it's more than just the nasty rumors you're spreading that have ended our association."

"What else has happened to make you fall out?" Alice asked. "Holly and I argued recently. It was all a big misunderstanding. Once I came to my senses, everything was sorted."

"Princess Alice, my senses are finely tuned," Professor Stephen said. "This situation is bigger than a mere misunderstanding. Wouldn't you say, Johann?"

Johann's hand shook as he picked up his glass. "We've been over this. I had no choice."

Alice leaned toward me. "What are they talking about?"

"I'm not sure. Why don't you find out?"

She walked over to Johann. "A good friend is hard to come by. Is there no way you can sort things out?"

Johann sighed. "I don't think so. Everything's a mess. My wife, Bethany, has taken everything. I don't even have anywhere to live."

"I tried to be sympathetic toward your situation, but that's your own fault," Professor Stephen said. "Your drinking is out of control. Bethany warned you several times to sort yourself out."

Johann's head lowered. "I thought I had a handle on things. I didn't realize I'd gotten in over my head."

Alice turned to me and widened her eyes.

I gestured for her to keep asking questions. Something big had gone down between these two, and it felt important.

"You must have been good friends for a long time," Alice said. "Are you sure you can't patch things up?"

"Would you want to be friends with someone who tried to blackmail you?" Professor Stephen said. "Because that's what my so-called friend has been doing."

"Goodness! I should say not," Alice said. "What was he blackmailing you about?"

"You just heard the lie straight from his mouth," Professor Stephen said. "The wild accusations that I've been stealing students' ideas and publishing them as my own. Of course, there's no truth in it. I mentor all my students. They may come up with the kernel of an idea, but

I work with them to develop it. And you can't patent an idea. Everybody knows that."

Alice glanced from Johann to Professor Stephen before stepping back to the table and pretending to study the cakes.

"I bet Professor Stephen doesn't give his students any credit when he publishes those papers," I muttered. "Ask him about that."

"If there's no truth to what I'm saying, why did you give me money?" Johann said.

Professor Stephen waved away the comment. "I felt sorry for you. I know what a desperate situation you're in. You could have asked for a loan, instead of blackmailing me. I'd have given you money to get you through this difficult time. Instead, you came creeping to my office and accused me of taking my students' work."

"I did ask for help," Johann said. "Several times. You just laughed and said you were a bit short that month. You said you'd just paid for three new dresses for Evelyn the last time I begged for help. I didn't want to keep pushing, but I had no other option."

"Why didn't you go to the police?" Alice asked Professor Stephen. "Blackmail is illegal. That would have stopped Johann."

Professor Stephen shifted from foot to foot. "I didn't want to see my old friend go to prison. He's a drunken idiot, but he doesn't deserve that."

"You didn't go to the police because you're guilty," Johann said. "I've had several students talk to me about their concerns over you taking their work."

"No doubt students who were unsuccessful as my assistants," Professor Stephen said. "I expect the very best from the students I take on. When they don't deliver, I let them go. That can leave a sour taste in the mouth. A taste that has them bending your ear and spreading lies about me."

"Or he's really been taking their work, and they feel powerless to do anything about it," I whispered to Alice.

"You're telling me you didn't think Ben was smart enough to assist you?" Johann asked.

"I never said that. What nonsense," Professor Stephen said. "Ben was an excellent assistant."

"Yet he came to me with his worries about you. Ben was concerned about the paper you were working on. It was full of his findings, yet every time he asked you about it, you brushed him off."

"Ben would never have spoken to you about such a sensitive matter." Bright dots of color appeared on Professor Stephen's cheeks.

I grabbed Alice's arm. This was the information I'd been missing. If Professor Stephen had stolen Ben's work, and he decided to expose him, it was the perfect motive for murder. Professor Stephen needed to keep Ben quiet, or his career would be over.

"Ben was planning to write to the University board about you," Johann said.

Alice squeaked and looked at me. "That's a motive."

I nodded and pressed a finger to my lips, focused on the men as they quarreled.

"You're a pathetic man," Professor Stephen said. "And I shall contact the University board as soon as I leave here. I'll recommend you're removed from your position. You're an embarrassment and a disgrace to the department. I should have done it a long time ago. My pity for you kept my mouth closed. Not anymore. Not now I know how swiftly you'd stab me in the back."

Johann staggered and grabbed the table. "You won't take my job from me. It's all I have."

"Try and stop me. You're finished."

Johann dropped his glass and lunged at Professor Stephen. They tumbled backward and landed on the floor before rolling around, grunting, yelling, and whacking at each other.

"What do you think about all of that?" Alice watched with wide eyes as the two men ineffectively wrestled.

"We've just heard a motive for Professor Stephen wanting Ben dead," I whispered.

"What about his injury? And his alibi?"

I pursed my lips. Those were two problems I hadn't figured out.

"Oomph! My back. Be careful, you idiot," Professor Stephen yelled.

Johann got Professor Stephen in a headlock, his face bright red. "You're a smug, overrated buffoon, who hasn't had a fresh thought since the Dark Ages."

"Gah! Help me." Professor Stephen held a hand out toward us.

The door to the drawing room opened. Campbell strode in. He took one look at the tussling men before glancing at me. "Well done, Holly. I'm sure this is exactly what you planned to happen."

I bit my bottom lip as Campbell pulled the two men apart. This afternoon party was supposed to help me find Johann's motive and pump him for useful information. Instead, I was looking straight at Professor Stephen again as the killer.

There had to be a way to figure out who killed Ben and Marcel. But at the moment, I was all out of ideas as to how to do that.

Chapter 18

As I folded flour into my devil's food cake mixture, I replayed the events of yesterday's party. I felt stuck, and didn't know which suspect to focus on.

Professor Stephen had a solid alibi for both murders, plus he was injured. And Johann had been too drunk to aim straight to get Ben, and he had Penny as an alibi for Marcel's death. Although double-checking he was actually with her would be wise.

Professor Stephen seemed more likely to be the killer, given he was stealing his students' work and passing it off as his own, but how had he managed it?

Then there was the thorny problem that Johann was a blackmailer, and a desperate one. He was on a dark path to ruin. Could that have led him to murder, as well?

I sighed as I folded and stirred the mixture. Much like this cake, this mystery felt like a big sticky mess.

I shook my head as I poured the rich, chocolate scented cake mixture into two tins, before sliding them into the oven and setting the timer.

"Holly, now you're done with that cake, Lady Philippa has asked for brunch in her room. It's already set out on that tray." Chef Heston pointed at the counter.

"Oh! Why don't you take it?"

"Are you giving me an order?" He arched a brow.

"Um, no. But you told me to be careful around the family. You know, not be their pet poodle."

He grunted. "I'm not taking the food. Besides, she asked for you, as usual."

"Does that mean you don't mind me being friendly with her?"

"It means I have better things to do than run around after the family all day. Get a move on before I assign you peeling duties."

I washed my hands. "The cake will be fine for thirty minutes. I'll go up now." I picked up the tray of smoked salmon bagels with cream cheese, fruit salad, and a pot of tea, and hurried out of the kitchen.

I slowed when I spotted Penny looking at an oil painting in the main hall.

She turned as I approached. "Hi, Holly. These pictures are so beautiful. They're way better than the cheap re-productions I have back home."

"Do you like oil paintings?"

"Some more than others," she said. "These are gorgeous."

"I heard you and Johann were looking at some of the art in the gallery the other evening."

She glanced at me. "You mean the evening Marcel was killed?"

I shrugged. "I didn't mean to be so obvious. It's just such a mystery. Why was he shot? And who did it?"

"It's a mystery why either Marcel or Ben were killed." Her eyes filled with tears. "I wish I knew who was behind this, but it wasn't Johann. He was with me. It's making me uneasy staying here, but the police insist I remain in the castle until everyone's been questioned. It doesn't feel safe, though. There could be someone out there picking us off one by one. What if I'm next?"

"You think someone wants you dead?" I said. "Have you been threatened?"

She twisted her hand together. "No, but it makes me nervous. I didn't think anyone would want to kill Ben, and look what happened to him. And then Marcel got an arrow in the back. He could be a bit of a whinger, but that's no reason to kill him."

"Why do you think Marcel was shot?" I asked. "Was he worried about anyone coming after him? Had he been threatened recently?"

"Not that I know of, but Marcel was a born worrier. He was always stressing about something. I don't think it helped that he always competed with Ben. He hid it well, but he was relieved that Ben was out of the picture. He'd hoped to step into his shoes and become Professor Stephen's main assistant." She blinked her shiny eyes. "You know, the more I think about it, the more Marcel looked good for Ben's murder. Now he's dead, I don't know what to believe, or who to trust."

It was as if Penny echoed my own thoughts. I'd been looking hard at Marcel for killing Ben, but now I was full of doubts about what was really going on.

"This will be resolved soon," I said. "The castle is safe. We have a great security team. If you look down the end of the corridor, one of them is lurking in the shadows, keeping an eye on us."

"It's a shame they weren't watching out for Ben and Marcel," Penny said. "And your security doesn't make me feel any better. I've seen enough longbow contests to know that an ace archer can be a long way from their target and still hit them." She glanced along the corridor. "And on that rather glum note, I think I'll stay in my room for the rest of the day. I've got plenty of books to keep me occupied, and I need to catch up on my latest paper."

"Try not to worry. I know this is a tough time for you. I bet you'll be able to leave any day now, and this will be resolved."

"I hope so. I don't feel like I can properly grieve for Ben until this has come to an end." Penny nodded at me before hurrying away.

I let out a sigh. I shared her confusion. This mystery was testing me. I didn't know which way to turn. I hated the thought of a killer getting away with this.

I hurried up the stone steps of the east turret, skipping swiftly past the cold spots and ignoring the disembodied whispers that always followed me up these stairs. I was in no mood for the castle ghosts today. Not when there was a real life scary mystery to solve.

I knocked on Lady Philippa's door before pushing it open.

Her overweight, grumpy corgi, Horatio, plodded over to me. He growled before circling me and sniffing the air.

"You leave Holly alone." Lady Philippa emerged from her bedroom. "I'm so glad you're here. I was about to faint with hunger. My family is negligent of my needs."

"I'm sure they'd have welcomed you at the breakfast table." I set down the tray.

"I doubt it. Some mad woman who predicted a nice young boy dying in our grounds would hardly be welcome," she said. "I know to take most of my meals up here and keep my mouth shut."

I suppressed a smile as I poured the tea and set out the food. That was the opposite of what Lady Philippa was really like. She always shared her thoughts and opinions with anyone within earshot.

"Sit down with me. Have a cup of tea," Lady Philippa said.

I did as I was told and took a sip of tea, my gaze going to the window.

"What's on your mind?" Lady Philippa said.

"Did you have a prediction about Marcel's murder?" I asked.

"Strangely not." Her hand strayed to the notebook on her side table. "I was only sure about Ben's murder. Although I had terrible indigestion the evening Marcel was shot. I should have realized that was a sign something bad would happen. Is that what's troubling you?"

I nodded. "It's all a bit of a mess. The prime suspect has an alibi, and I've hit a brick wall. Most of the suspects have been ruled out."

"Who's your prime suspect?"

"It was Marcel, then he got killed. I was interested in Johann, but he has alibis for both murders. Now, I'm looking at Professor Stephen—"

"He was the chap giving the lecture when I had my premonition about Ben," Lady Philippa said.

"That's right. He has the perfect motive for wanting Ben dead. According to Johann, he's been stealing his students' ideas and publishing them as his own. It's funny, I always wondered how he came up with such unusual theories. He jumps from one topic to another so easily. Now, it's obvious. They were never his ideas in the first place."

"Do you trust Johann?"

"I think so. Although his life's chaotic and he was blackmailing Professor Stephen."

"He sounds utterly untrustworthy."

"Neither of them are angels. Professor Stephen has been abusing his power. His students know they can't complain about him. If anyone went up against him, they wouldn't be taken seriously, and their career would be over before it began."

"He doesn't sound like a nice man," Lady Philippa said.

"I agree, but he got injured in the shooting contest, and he was with his wife when both murders happened. It wasn't him. That doesn't leave anyone else."

"You're absolutely sure?" Lady Philippa said.

"It can't be Penny, Ben's girlfriend. She doesn't know how to shoot. Plus, she was with Johann when Marcel was shot. There's Evelyn, Professor Stephen's wife, but she was with him on both occasions and she also doesn't shoot. There's the tech guy, Eddie, but he alibied out. Plus, he's no longer in the castle. He left with the rest of the work crew."

Lady Philippa finished her bagel and wiped her hands on a napkin. "I have an idea that could help you figure this out. Do you have pictures of the remaining suspects?"

"I'm sure I can find pictures of Professor Stephen and Johann online. Why do you want to see them?"

"By looking at their faces, I may be able to divine which one of them is guilty."

"You can do that?" I pulled out my phone and searched for images of Professor Stephen and Johann.

"I've never done it before, but I had a strong connection to Ben. I feel involved in this murder. We must make sure his killer is found."

"That's exactly what I want. Here you go, this is a picture of Johann." I handed my phone to Lady Philippa.

She looked at it for several seconds before closing her eyes and placing her hand over the screen.

"Are you sensing anything?" I leaned forward and stared at her.

"Give me a moment." She sat back in her seat and breathed deeply.

I took a sip of my tea. I wasn't sure if I believed in her abilities, but I'd try anything to figure out who the killer was.

"I don't think it was him." Lady Philippa passed back my phone. "I'm getting no bad feelings. Although there is an air of desperation about that man."

"You can't tell that through a picture," I said.

"Are you suggesting I'm wrong?" She arched an eyebrow. "I'm really just a mad old woman locked in a turret."

"No! But, I mean, that's amazing if you really can do that. Johann's lost everything. He's drinking too much, his wife has left him, and he's got nowhere to live. And Professor Stephen is threatening to take his job."

"There you go. Maybe I can sense things through pictures, after all. Show me a picture of Professor Stephen."

I hurriedly pulled up a picture of him. It looked like it had been taken at a shooting competition. He stood outside, a bright green lawn behind him and a bow in his hand.

Lady Philippa took my phone again and went through the same process of touching the screen and deep breathing.

"What do you think of him?" I asked.

"Deceitful. I could well believe he'd steal his students' work. But there's something else about this image. It's not connected to him, but someone is unbalanced." She removed her hand from the screen and stared at it. "What you have here is a deeply unpleasant individual. But I wouldn't mark Professor Stephen as your killer."

I took my phone back and expanded the picture, looking at everyone else in it. Evelyn stood beside Professor Stephen, holding the medal he must have won and smiling at him. I scrolled down the page and read the text underneath.

I jumped from my seat, my body going hot and cold in alternating swirls of disbelief. "Are you kidding me?"

Horatio yipped and glared at me.

"What have you found?" Lady Philippa's eyes gleamed with interest.

"Evelyn Maguire. She lied. She's holding a medal in this picture. I assumed it had been won by Professor Stephen. It says here that she won a gold medal for archery. She told me she didn't shoot." I quickly searched for more records for Evelyn Maguire and longbow contests. Sure enough, she'd won places in numerous competitions going back over two decades.

"Don't keep me in suspense," Lady Philippa said. "What else have you found?"

"Professor Stephen and Evelyn met at a shooting contest. She's been shooting longer than he has." I looked up at her. "I overlooked her. She seemed like such a sweet lady. I believed Evelyn when she said she didn't know how to shoot."

"That must have been who I was sensing when I looked at that picture," Lady Philippa said. "Her mind is unbalanced and dark."

I shook my head. "I've been such an idiot. I let all that nonsense about women being less effective archers sink in and influence me during this investigation. I didn't even realize what I was doing."

"Alice is an excellent shooter. You know that."

"I do! I absolutely know that! I've seen her shoot plenty of times. I got swayed by what everyone else was telling me."

"Well, you're not swayed anymore. What are you going to do?" Lady Philippa said.

I stared at the picture of Evelyn. "Did he cover for his wife, or was it the other way round? It must have been one of them. Either Professor Stephen or Evelyn murdered Ben and Marcel."

"You need to get out of here and find out exactly which one fired those arrows."

I was already heading to the door, my heartbeat matching my rapid steps. "Thanks, Lady Philippa."

"You can thank me by getting a killer out of my castle."

I nodded. That's exactly what I planned to do.

Chapter 19

After promising Lady Philippa that I'd keep her informed about what was going on, I raced down the east turret staircase. I had to tell Campbell what I'd discovered about Evelyn. Right now, a former superspy on my side was just what I needed.

I hunted around the castle for ten minutes, but there was no sign of him on the ground floor. I raced up to the first floor. That was weird. There was no security around. It was like they'd vanished.

"Holly, are you looking for someone?" Rupert ambled along the corridor, his hands in his pockets.

"Campbell. Well, actually anyone from the security team will do right now."

"I can help you with that. They're all at the top secret weekly debrief," Rupert said. "They've disappeared for an hour to plot out the security measures for the next seven days."

"Why did they have to do that now?" I groaned. The security team changed the day and time they met every week so there was never a predictable pattern to their movements, but the timing couldn't be worse.

"Is there anything I can assist you with?" He ran a hand through his hair. "You look a bit flustered."

I stared at Rupert for several seconds. Should I get him involved? Campbell would skin me alive if he found out I was including another member of the family in the business of solving murders.

"I'd really like to help," he said. "Whatever you need, I'm all yours."

"I need backup," I said. "And I need a way to get the remaining suspects for Ben and Marcel's murders together. I think I know who killed them. Can you help with that?"

"That's no problem," Rupert said. "We all had a late breakfast this morning. Everyone was in the dining room when I left five minutes ago. If we hurry, we can catch them all there."

"That's perfect. Let's go now."

Rupert walked beside me as I hurried along the corridor and back down the stairs. "Are you going to let me in on who you think the killer is?"

"Of course!" I needed Rupert to know what he was getting himself into. "These murders are linked to reputation. It was either Professor Stephen or Evelyn who killed Ben and Marcel, to make sure his job was safe."

Rupert's eyes widened. "It can't have been Evelyn. She's such a kind woman. She's barely left her husband's side since he was injured. That's not the behavior of a cold-hearted killer."

"I thought the same. When we met, Evelyn charmed me. She also lied about her ability to use a longbow."

"What about the blackmail angle? Alice said Johann was taking money from Stephen."

"That's true, but if the motive for murder was blackmail, Professor Stephen would have shot Johann."

Rupert rubbed his chin. "I'm still not certain Evelyn has anything to do with this."

"Maybe there's a good reason she's not left Professor Stephen's side," I said. "What if she killed Ben and Marcel and asked him to cover for her? She'd need to keep a close eye on him to make sure he stuck to his end of the deal."

"Or she's covering for him."

"That's my dilemma. Which one of them did it?" I said. "Which is why we have to confront them together. If I reveal what I know, whoever is covering may let something slip to save their own skin."

"I've got your back. I'll help in any way I can." Rupert gave my arm a reassuring squeeze before opening the dining room door for me.

"Oh, good." Professor Stephen gestured me over. "I need more coffee."

I ignored him as he waved his cup at me, relieved to see Evelyn, Penny, and Johann were still at the table.

"Holly's not here to bring you coffee," Rupert said. "She has some very important questions for you."

"Oh! Lord Rupert. I didn't see you there." Professor Stephen's brows lowered. "What kind of questions? Does she work for you?"

Rupert nodded at me. "In a way. Whenever you're ready, Holly."

I looked at the people sitting at the table before clearing my throat and rolling my shoulders. "Someone in this room killed Ben and Marcel."

There was a collective gasp.

"And how do you know that?" Professor Stephen said. "Did you see the murders take place?"

"No, but I've spoken to all the suspects, and—"

"Hold on. Why are you even investigating this?" Professor Stephen asked. "You don't look like a member of the household security."

"Holly is practically a member of this family," Rupert said. "She's cleverer than all of us put together."

"Thanks, Lord Rupert," I said.

"She's not smarter than me," Professor Stephen muttered.

"Actually, she's pretty clever. Holly helped me in my hour of need," Johann said.

"That's no surprise, since you need all the help you can get," Professor Stephen said.

It looked like their feud was still unresolved.

"Let Holly continue," Rupert said.

Professor Stephen gestured at me, his eyes narrowed. "As you wish, Lord Rupert."

I looked him in the eye. "I think either you or your wife killed Ben and Marcel."

There was another collective gasp. Penny dropped her knife, Johann snorted coffee across the table, and Professor Stephen's face paled.

Evelyn blinked rapidly. She looked at her husband. "Stephen, did you do something bad?"

"Me! I didn't have anything to do with the murders," he said. "This is an outrageous accusation."

"Holly, are you sure about this?" Penny's face was ghost-white as she looked at Professor Stephen.

"I am," I said. "Professor Stephen was being blackmailed by Johann because he was stealing students' work and passing it off as his own. Isn't that true?" I looked over at Johann.

He shifted in his seat. "It is. It's not something I'm proud of, but I had no choice. And I have evidence to support what he's been doing."

Penny sucked in a breath. "That was why Ben was so stressed before he was killed. He kept saying there was a problem, and he didn't know how to solve it. I had a feeling it had something to do with Professor Stephen, but he told me he was dealing with it. And Ben was talking about finding a new mentor. I couldn't understand it at the time."

"None of these nonsense accusations will stick," Professor Stephen said. "Even if it turns out I accidentally used some of my students' research, it would be a simple misunderstanding, and easy to clear up. I wouldn't kill because of it."

"I'm not so sure about that," Johann said. "Your job would be on the line, as would your reputation."

"Rubbish. I'm what makes that history department. There's no way they'd get rid of me."

Penny threw her napkin down. "You stole Ben's research! Is that why you killed him? He was going to reveal what you were doing."

Everyone turned and stared at Professor Stephen, including Evelyn.

He tugged at the collar of his shirt. "I'm clever enough not to have to steal anyone else's work. This is a ridiculous theory by some headstrong young woman who doesn't know what she's talking about."

"I know enough to be convinced that you're involved in this," I said. "You and your wife."

Evelyn shook her head. "No, not me. I'd never hurt anyone. I liked Ben and Marcel."

"And I was injured at the shooting contest," Professor Stephen said. "I can't shoot without being in agony."

"Maybe you're not as badly hurt as you've made out you are," I said.

"I've been examined by a doctor," he said. "And my injury was made worse thanks to that ridiculous chair Princess Alice made me sit on. I can assure you, none of this has been faked."

"Darling, you're starting to worry me," Evelyn said. "You really are hurt, aren't you?"

"I'm also worried about why you lied." I turned my attention to Evelyn. "You know how to shoot a longbow."

She took a sip of tea before lowering her cup. "I do, but that was a long time ago. I haven't fired a bow for years. I'm out of practice. I had nothing to do with those young men's deaths."

"You've won medals for your shooting in longbow competitions," I said. "There are articles about you online. You don't forget a skill like that."

Professor Stephen glanced at Evelyn. "You did go away for a long weekend shooting with some friends not so long ago."

Her eyes narrowed. "That was just for fun. And I wasn't very good. I'm certainly not good enough to have shot Ben or Marcel. You, however, are an excellent shot. You're always telling people how good you are."

I listened to them bicker for a few seconds. The solid relationship they presented when in public was already crumbling.

"You said you were together when both murders happened." I addressed the question to Evelyn.

She nodded. "I was with Stephen in the woods, helping him to the castle after he hurt his back. And we were together in our room when Marcel was shot."

"Are you certain you were together the whole time?" I asked.

"That's correct," she said.

Professor Stephen cleared his throat. "Well, I mean—"

"Shush, darling," Evelyn said. "We were together. That's the end of the story."

No, it wasn't. Evelyn was eerily calm about this whole situation and had been quick to throw suspicion at her husband by questioning his injury. "Maybe you're covering for Professor Stephen. I understand if you are. How long have you been married?"

"Almost twenty years," Evelyn said after a long pause.

"You wouldn't want to see him get in trouble," I said. "It can't feel good to be married to a man who has committed murder."

"Not only that, but he's a liar and a cheat," Johann said.

"I'm none of those things." Professor Stephen gripped the edge of the table. "Evelyn, tell them. I didn't do this."

She glanced at him, and her shoulders lifted an inch. "There's no proof either of us killed Ben or Marcel. You can't charge us with anything."

Rupert stepped up beside me and leaned down so his mouth was by my ear. "I've got an idea. I'll get the truth out of them."

I shot him a curious look. What was he going to do?

Rupert walked closer to the table. "If these murders are related to the whole blackmail issue, I'll have my security access your financial records. That'll show us exactly what's been going on."

Everyone's expression turned confused, and I winced and shook my head. I didn't think blackmail was the motivator in these crimes.

"Did Ben ask for money in exchange for his silence?" Rupert asked Professor Stephen.

"No! Ben was an honest, hardworking student," Professor Stephen said.

Rupert glanced at me, panic flaring in his eyes. "Then it was you, Johann. You wanted more money. Remember, I can check if you're lying."

I bit my lip. Maybe I shouldn't have gotten Rupert involved in this, after all. He was steering the questioning in the wrong direction and taking the spotlight away from Evelyn and Professor Stephen.

"I've already admitted I was taking money from Stephen because I was desperate," Johann said. "Why would I kill Ben and Marcel because Stephen wouldn't give me more money?"

Rupert waved a hand in the air as if conducting an orchestra only he could see. "I... well, someone in here is a killer. And I'll get my team on it straight away to see about those dubious financial records. Holly, back to you." He returned to my side, his shoulders slumped.

I appreciated his efforts, but those questions had gotten us exactly nowhere.

Professor Stephen shrugged. "You can check what you like, Lord Rupert. You'll see I had no more money to give away. In fact, I'm heading along the same path as Johann."

Johann's expression grew puzzled. "How is that possible? I never asked you for an outrageous amount of money, only enough to get by on. I understand you don't make a fortune being a lecturer, even with your book sales, but you can't be in debt."

Professor Stephen licked his lips and glanced at his wife. "You're not my only financial drain."

Evelyn set her cup down. "That's your own fault. You never were any good with money, darling."

For someone whose husband was being accused of two murders, she was still playing it cool. There was zero sign she was worried about him going to prison.

Johann jumped from his seat and strode over to Professor Stephen. "I regret blackmailing you. I let my desperation get the better of me. I should have put our friendship first. Can you forgive me?"

Professor Stephen grabbed Johann's outstretched hand. "Of course. I should have offered to help you. I knew you were having trouble. And I never trusted that wife of yours."

"You warned me not to marry her," Johann said. "I was blinded by what I thought was true love. She changed as soon as we married. She kept demanding more until I ran out of ways to make her happy. I began drinking because it helped blot out my panic and eased the stress. That only made my wife hate me. Before I knew it, she'd thrown me out and changed the locks. I panicked. I made a huge mistake."

"As did I. We'll always be friends. I spoke out of anger earlier. Your job is safe. You have nothing to worry about."

The men embraced and patted each other on the back.

My attention was only half on them as Evelyn sat silently in her seat, her expression blank.

"Professor Stephen, I don't understand what you meant about having more than one financial drain," I said.

He glanced at me. "What's that got to do with you?"

"Answer her question," Rupert said. "It's important to Ben and Marcel's murders."

Professor Stephen cleared his throat and glanced at his wife again. "It's a personal matter. I'm dealing with it."

My eyes widened. "Evelyn is blackmailing you, too?"

Rupert stood beside me, his expression sharp. "Answer Holly. And remember, we have ways to check these things."

I nodded, grateful now for Rupert's assistance. "Is that why you gave her a fake alibi for the murders?"

"My alibis aren't fake," Evelyn said. "Stephen hurt himself at the shooting contest. He wouldn't have been able to walk back to the castle without me helping him. We were together."

"Professor Stephen?" I asked. "Were you with Evelyn the whole time in the woods that afternoon?"

"I, um, well, I mean…" He stumbled over several more half-formed words.

"Not another sound," Evelyn said. "We were together."

"What has Evelyn got on you that makes you afraid to reveal the truth?" I said.

Johann patted Professor Stephen on the arm. "It's best if it all comes out. Has this got to do with your latest research project?"

Evelyn tutted and shook her head. "You're as bad as each other. You're only interested in the past. Can't you see how tedious that is for the rest of us? No wonder your wife kicked you out, Johann. Some of us look to the future. We need to make plans."

"What plans do you have for the future that meant you had to blackmail your husband?" I said.

"I've not confirmed that I blackmailed Stephen," Evelyn said.

"I told you this had to do with blackmail," Rupert whispered to me.

"It's all going to come out in the end, especially when the finances get looked into," Professor Stephen said quietly.

"It isn't, if you keep your mouth shut," Evelyn said, all sweetness fading from her face as her shoulders stiffened. She stood from her seat, her hands clenched.

Johann nodded at Professor Stephen. "Let's get this sorry business finished. Ben and Marcel were decent young men. They deserve justice."

I nodded at him. My thoughts exactly.

Professor Stephen swallowed and patted his chest, before glancing at me. "I'm not sure how you figured it all out, but Evelyn's been robbing me blind."

"Keep quiet," she said through gritted teeth. "I'm your wife. I'm not robbing you blind. You should take care of me. It's your responsibility as my husband."

"Does she have evidence that you stole work from your students, too?" I asked.

"No, this isn't about my work. It's about the fundraising events Evelyn puts on to raise money for the department. I sign off on the final income. And, well, I may have taken some money for… administrative expenses." Professor Stephen ducked his head.

"You stole money from a fundraising event," I said. "What did you need it for?"

"For Evelyn," he whispered.

"I never asked you to do that," Evelyn said. "This has nothing to do with me."

"Stephen," Johann said, his tone reproachful. "Those people gave you that money to further historical research."

"You can keep quiet." Evelyn's knuckles cracked as she pressed them on the table. "You're a washed up drunk and a blackmailer."

"Evelyn found out what I was doing," Professor Stephen said, his voice so low I could barely hear him. "At first, she joked about it and said I'd have to give her a gift to keep her quiet. I didn't think she was being serious. After all, we're a partnership. We look out for each other. Then the joking ended, and the demands started. I was in over my head. I was just about managing when Johann came along and threatened to expose what I was doing with my students' work."

"My dear friend, I'm so sorry to put you in a tight spot," Johann said.

"I don't blame you," Professor Stephen said. "You couldn't have known my wife was holding this over my head."

"You're making a big mistake." Evelyn's cheeks were pinched and her eyes tight. "This is a private matter. Why tell anyone else about this?"

"You're the one who made the mistake," I said. "You shot Ben and Marcel and expected your husband to cover for you. Professor Stephen, were you with Evelyn when the murders took place?"

His head whipped around to his wife. "No! You left me in the woods."

"To grab my keys. I left them behind at the shooting range. I've already told you that."

I shook my head. "That's not true. You never came back to the shooting range after Professor Stephen got injured."

"I didn't have to. I was walking back when I found them in my pocket. I was barely gone for five minutes." She bared her teeth and stepped away from the table. "Why would I want to kill Ben?"

"Because he threatened to go public about Professor Stephen's theft of his work," I said. "Ben must have felt so conflicted about whether to reveal what he knew. Here was a man he greatly admired, but Professor Stephen was also a thief."

"That's true," Penny said. "Ben was battling with a problem he wouldn't share with me."

I nodded. "You became worried about him, Evelyn. If Ben revealed what Professor Stephen was doing, it would have ended his career and your opportunity to blackmail him. There'd be no more fundraisers to skim money off. You had to make sure that didn't happen."

"Tell me this isn't true," Professor Stephen said, his wide-eyed stare fixed on Evelyn. "You killed Ben for money?"

She shook her head, her ice-cold gaze shifting around the room. "You think you're so clever, but you're an idiot. You signed off on those fundraising accounts without giving them a second glance."

Professor Stephen sputtered and color flooded his cheeks. "You always tell me you don't have a head for figures. I was doing you a favor by checking through the books and making sure everything was in order."

"If you knew how to read a set of accounts properly, you'd have seen an expense line that shouldn't have been there," Evelyn said.

"You were stealing from the fundraising events and blackmailing your husband for even more money?" I'd been so fooled by the sweet facade Evelyn had in place.

She smirked. "Why not? Stephen put me in the category of his good, simple wife. The pretty little thing he could have on his arm and parade around at events. I was never any trouble and never questioned him. I'd smile and laugh in all the right places to make him look good. On the inside, I was dying of boredom. The first time I set up a fundraising event, I had no idea how much money it would bring in. When I saw the bottom line, I couldn't resist taking a little."

"Evelyn!" Professor Stephen shook his head. "How could you?"

"Oh, be quiet. You were doing the same," Evelyn said. "I realized how simple it was to take what I wanted. Stephen was too wrapped up in his boring work to notice. I needed my freedom. Having that money tucked away meant I could escape when it became too much for me."

"You wanted to escape from me?" Professor Stephen took a step back, his hand going to his chest. "I thought we were happy."

"Exactly! You thought that. You never bothered to ask me what I wanted. You've never once asked me if I was happy being a stay-at-home housewife, not having a career, not being blessed with the children I desired, having to listen to your endless dirge about the dull happenings in the history department. History is in the past. That's where it needs to stay."

Professor Stephen opened and closed his mouth several times, but nothing came out.

"What about Marcel?" I said.

Evelyn crossed her arms over her chest. "What about him? He was another puffed up know-it-all who needed to be put in his place."

"Enough! I'm not covering for you, anymore." Professor Stephen's face grew red. "Evelyn is guilty. She left me alone for ten minutes on the night of Marcel's shooting. You said you went to the library to grab a book. I thought it was a bit strange, given the number of books we'd brought with us."

Evelyn shrugged. "Marcel was an unfortunate casualty. I thought I'd gotten away with shooting Ben. In fact, I almost didn't need to bother firing that arrow at all. Marcel had his own plan for getting rid of Ben."

I gasped. "The partial print that was found on the arrow in the woods. Marcel tried to shoot Ben at the same time as you."

She snorted a laugh. "You're right. I couldn't believe my luck when I saw him aim an arrow at Ben. I stood and watched, waiting for him to take Ben out and solve my worries. But the idiot was shaking. There was no way he'd make the shot with a tremble in his hand."

"And he missed Ben," I said, glancing at Rupert. "That was the arrow Meatball discovered on the day of the shooting."

She nodded. "It landed a couple of feet away from Ben. So, I took my shot and finished the job."

"But you became worried that Marcel had seen what you did," I said.

"I wasn't at first, but he asked to see me. He said he had some important information I needed to know about. I could only think it was one thing. I decided Marcel wouldn't get the chance to weasel his way into my life. So, I arranged to meet him outside. Then all I needed to do was get my timing right. I watched him wander out onto the lawn. It was like he was begging me to shoot him. He stood there in a bright white shirt."

"Evelyn, you're a monster," Professor Stephen said.

"It takes one to know one, darling," Evelyn said. "I'm barely living a life, confined as your wife, no prospects, no career, and no children to occupy my time. I'm quite certain that life behind bars will be much more entertaining than trailing after you like the dull, dutiful wife you turned me into. Although I suspect you may get to see time behind bars too, since you're basically a liar and a thief."

"Now, hold on a moment. Let's not be too hasty." Professor Stephen's gaze darted around the room. "I took a little money. I didn't kill two people."

"We should let the police decide what happens to you both," I said. "Lord Rupert, perhaps you could—"

Evelyn shrieked and lunged toward Rupert. There was a glint of something silver in her right hand as she raised her arm.

My gaze shot to Rupert. He was standing there, his mouth open as Evelyn drew nearer. He didn't even raise an arm to protect himself.

I threw myself on top of Rupert, knocking him out of Evelyn's path. A spark of pain flared through my left arm as we flew through the air.

I smacked down on top of Rupert, my knees protesting as they skimmed across the carpet.

Rupert let out a grunt, his breath shooting out of him as he hit the floor.

I lifted my head and stared down at him. I was straddled across his chest, my cleavage shoved in his face. "Are you okay?"

He gave a small nod, his nose bumping into my chest as he did so. "Are you?"

"Fine." I rolled off him and jumped to my feet.

Professor Stephen and Johann had restrained Evelyn. A knife from the table lay at her feet.

I blinked as I studied the knife. That wasn't strawberry preserve on the knife blade. I whirled back to Rupert. Had she injured him?

"Holly, your arm!" Rupert grabbed my shoulder. "You're bleeding."

I looked back at the knife and then at the slash through my shirt where Evelyn had stabbed me. "I'm okay. I feel…" The room spun and black dots filled my vision.

"Grab her. She's going down," Professor Stephen said, his voice foggy as I struggled to breathe.

"No, really, I'm…"

Chapter 20

I sat up with a jerk, gasping in a breath. Had that been a vivid dream, or did Evelyn just stab me with a butter knife?

I moved my head. My cheek was pressed against a satin cushion. This wasn't the floor of the dining room I'd been flailing about on a moment ago.

Warm, firm hands grabbed mine, and Rupert's face appeared. "You're okay. You fainted. But you're safe. No one's going to hurt you."

A shudder ran down my spine as the events in the dining room clicked into place. "Evelyn, where is she?"

"She's gone. She can't get anywhere near you." Alice raced through the door, ran to the couch I lay on, and flung her arms around me.

"Careful of her arm," Rupert said.

When Alice pulled back, her cheeks were wet with tears. "When I heard what happened, I thought I was going to lose you. My best friend murdered by the family silverware." She hugged me again.

I tried to hug her back, but an aching throb in my right arm meant I could only feebly pat her with one hand.

A quick glance around showed me we were in one of the private family rooms. "I'm a bit fuzzy on the details if anyone wants to fill me in."

Rapid, frantic barking came from the corridor. A few seconds later, Meatball bounded through the door. He launched himself onto my chest before sniffing all around my face and licking my cheek several times.

"How did you get in here?" I asked, grateful to have my best furry buddy squashing me. After almost being stabbed, I was in need of comforting.

"I let him in," Alice said. "He was barking like crazy outside. He knew you were in danger."

"I'm fine." I scratched between his ears. "None of you have anything to worry about."

Meatball planted himself on my chest and refused to move, his large dark eyes fixed on mine.

"Do you need anything?" Alice asked as she hovered around me. "Maybe we should take you to the hospital."

"I don't think I need to go to the hospital," I said. "Although my arm does hurt. How long was I passed out?"

"Twenty minutes," Rupert said.

I looked at the bandage around my left arm. "Did you do this?"

"No, that was Campbell," Rupert said.

I struggled to sit up, clasping Meatball against my chest with my uninjured arm. "Tell me everything. I remember Evelyn confessing to both murders, then I suggested Rupert get the police. That was when she lunged."

Rupert scrubbed at his forehead with his fingers. "It all happened so fast. After Evelyn tried to stab me, and you fainted, it went crazy."

"The last thing I recall, we were getting up from the floor, and Professor Stephen and Johann were holding Evelyn."

"That's right. Ten seconds later, Campbell charged through the door," Rupert said. "One of his security team alerted him to a problem when he heard a scream from the dining room."

"That must have been Evelyn, just before she ran at you," I said.

He nodded. "Campbell came in, saw you were injured, saw the bloody knife, and removed you from the scene. Stephen and Johann came with us and confirmed Evelyn's confession."

I let out a long slow breath. "Then what?"

"Campbell's team took Evelyn to the police station. Stephen's gone with her. He promised not to hold anything back. The blackmail, the theft, the cover up, it'll all come out."

"And Johann and Penny?"

"He's waiting to be questioned, as is Penny," Rupert said. "They'll support our side of the story."

"I can't believe Evelyn did that. I wish I'd been there. I'd have karate chopped her and stopped that evil witch getting near either of you." Alice grasped my hand. "You saved my brother's life. He might be a nitwit of epic proportions, but I don't want anyone stabbing him."

Rupert patted my shoulder. "Holly was so brave. I just stood there, too scared to move. She didn't hesitate and threw herself on me. She risked her life to keep me safe."

"I, um, well, I didn't really think about what I was doing." Would I sacrifice myself for Rupert? I liked him, a lot more than I should, given my position, but would I die by sword, or butter knife, to ensure his survival? "I saw the knife, and that Evelyn was heading straight for you, and just reacted."

"You're our hero," Alice said. "You should receive a knighthood for this."

"She's not a hero." Campbell stalked into the room, his shoulders tight and close to his ears. "She's an idiot. She could have been killed."

"Hey! That's hardly fair," I said. "You can't be angry with me. I was doing your job. I helped to find the killer and protect Lord Rupert. Where were you? Having tea and cookies with your team while discussing your diaries for the week."

Campbell's eyes narrowed. "I warned you something like this would happen. You kept poking your nose in this investigation, goading the killer into striking out at you."

"I'm glad she did," Alice said. "Holly solved two murders, discovered a blackmail ring, learned about some illicit business with money I don't quite understand, and saved my brother's life. Like I said, she should get a knighthood."

"She's a woman," Campbell said, his tone unusually terse as he addressed Alice. "They don't get knighthoods. They become Dames."

"Then it's time for a change in the law," Alice said. "I know several members in the House of Lords. They'll put in a good word for me. Don't worry, Holly. We'll get you a medal for bravery." She winked at me.

"And I'll forever be in your debt," Rupert said to me.

"There's no need for that," I said.

"You only got a flesh wound," Campbell said. "And my team was on the verge of figuring out what was going on with Evelyn and Stephen. I'd been looking into Professor Stephen's financial records and those of his wife. There were unusual transactions going on, including an offshore bank account with a traceable origin."

"And that account traced to Evelyn?" I said.

"That's the direction the information was taking us," Campbell said.

"None of that is important," Alice said. "Holly got the confession out of Evelyn before she tried to kill Rupert. Your evidence is old hat, Campbell."

I bit my bottom lip, sort of loving how red Campbell was turning. I decided to throw him a lifeline. "That evidence will be useful when the case goes to court. Evelyn's confession is important, but there wasn't much physical evidence at either crime scene."

"You don't say," Campbell said.

I smiled sweetly at his sharpness, feeling a bit buzzed from all the adrenaline still pumping through me.

"Holly, I'll need a statement from you," Campbell said.

"She's too weak to give a statement," Alice said. "She needs a month off work and zero stress."

"I'm sure I'll be fine to get back to work," I said. "I don't want any fuss. My arm's already feeling better." I attempted to flex my bicep and almost passed out again.

"Even though it was a flesh wound, that knife was sharp," Campbell said, his tone softening. "I won't need your statement right away. Get a couple of days rest, and then we'll talk." He nodded at Alice and Rupert before leaving the room.

"He's such a grump. Just because you were the hero of the day and solved the case, he's taking it out on us," Alice said.

"Campbell doesn't like me sticking my nose in his business," I said.

"I insist you keep doing just that. If it weren't for you, I'd have no brother." Alice tilted her head. "Actually, that's not a bad idea. With Rupert out the way, I'd get first crack at the breakfast pastries every morning."

Rupert swatted her arm and grinned. "Murdered for pastries. That would be a scandal."

I smiled as Rupert and Alice bickered. Finally, the castle felt safe again.

"What can we do to help you?" Alice said as she turned back to me. "Anything. You name it, and we'll get it sorted. Nothing is too much trouble."

"All I want to do is lay down for a bit. Although a cup of tea would be good."

"Tea! Why didn't I think of that?" Alice shoved Rupert. "Get Holly some tea."

"Of course." He jumped to his feet before grabbing my hand and kissing it. "Once again, thank you. I'll never forget what you did for me today."

I lay back on the couch, cuddling Meatball close to me. I took in a few deep breaths and zoned out as Alice talked about my bravery and how wonderful I was.

In truth, I really hadn't been thinking. I could have frozen to the spot just like Rupert. I still wasn't sure why I'd flung myself on top of him. I guess I wanted to keep Lord Rupert in my life.

I kissed Meatball on the head before closing my eyes. Even so, that had been a bit too close for comfort for my liking. The next time I decided to act like a hero, I may just shout for Campbell to step up, instead. After all, wasn't that what he got paid to do?

※※※※※ ※※※※※

"Are you sure you're well enough to walk?" Rupert hovered next to me, one hand behind my back, not quite touching, but so close that the warmth radiated through my sweater.

"I feel fine," I said. "Two days of resting in bed is more than enough for me. And it was my arm that was injured, not my legs. I'm used to getting regular exercise. Being inside any longer will send me stir crazy. A walk around Audley St. Mary is just what I need."

"You just say if you want to rest," Rupert said. "I'm right here. I'll even carry you if you think that would help."

I smiled and ignored the tickle of irritation inside me. Rupert had barely left my side in two days, only leaving to let me sleep and shower. It was like he was my personal bodyguard. It was sweet of him, but also incredibly stifling, because wherever Rupert went, Campbell was hovering close by, like a huge, smoldering, angry shadow.

Rupert had driven us into the village, insisting I wasn't strong enough to walk, and we were taking a gentle stroll along the quiet streets.

The sun felt amazing on my skin after being inside for two days. Meatball was by my side, happy to be out and about with me.

The last two days, Alice had insisted on taking him out, and I'd missed our walks together.

I was glad life was getting back to normal. Although being stabbed made me question things. Maybe I should stop being so reckless and poking around in the mysteries at the castle. I could only be lucky so many times before it ran out. And as Campbell kept predicting, something bad would happen. He'd been right this time. If Evelyn had been a few inches to the left with that knife, I wouldn't be walking anywhere ever again.

"Look! Your old store is having a 'make your own pot' event in three weeks' time," Rupert said. "I've never tried pottery. That could be fun."

We stopped outside my former café. The front had been repainted, and a new sign was above the door. Artfully Homewares.

I patted the window frame. "I'll have to drop by. I still haven't met the owner." I needed to make sure that whoever was looking after my store was taking excellent care of it.

"We could meet the owner together," Rupert said. "How about we sign up for the make your own pot course together?"

"That sounds nice," I said. "Maybe making a pot is like baking bread. You have to follow the exact steps or it'll collapse. I could be good at pottery."

"I'm sure you will be." He cleared his throat. "Then it's a date."

My eyes widened, and I stared up at him. That wasn't a light-hearted tone. "Like a date, date?"

A red flush crept up his cheeks and into his hairline. "Well, you did save my life. It's the least I can do."

"Rupert, for the last time, I didn't save your life. I doubt a butter knife would really kill a person."

"You never know, Evelyn was moving fast. And I saw murder glinting in those crazed eyes of hers."

"Panic, fear, maybe a little craziness at being trapped in a life she no longer wanted, but she wouldn't have killed you," I said.

He gazed up into the late afternoon sunshine. "I'm just glad she's been charged with double murder and embezzlement. We won't ever have to see her again. And now everyone from the history party has gone home, the castle is back to its old self."

"I doubt things will be the same for Professor Stephen," I said. "Is there any news on what's happening with him?" I turned as someone loudly and obviously cleared their throat. I tried not to roll my eyes, but it was a struggle, as I spotted Campbell lurking close by.

He gave me a small shake of his head. I knew what that meant. Stop prying.

I grinned at him, ignoring the warning look in his eyes. "Campbell, do you have something to say?"

His mouth tightened before he nodded. "If I may, Lord Rupert?"

"Of course. Go ahead," Rupert said. "What's the latest news?"

"The University board has dismissed Professor Stephen from his position," Campbell said. "They've decided not to press charges regarding his theft, providing he repays the money. In addition, any work he published that wasn't his own is being withdrawn from publication and returned to its original owners. Of course, those individuals may decide to sue Professor Stephen in a private court case, that's yet to be decided. Stephen's career as a lecturer is over. He'll be lucky if he gets a teaching job in a local night school."

"That's no more than he deserves," Rupert said. "Actually, it's more than he deserves. He exploited his students and took money that wasn't his. He's lucky not to be in prison."

"He got off lightly," Campbell said. "It seems the University didn't want a scandal that could taint their reputation and deter future donors."

"He didn't get off that lightly. He is married to a double murderer," I said. "That's a harsh punishment to live with."

Campbell nodded. "On that, we agree."

"There you all are." Alice trotted around the corner and hurried over, her own security not far behind. "Holly, I couldn't believe it when I came to your apartment and found it empty. Then I discovered that Rupert took you out without asking if I wanted to come along." She smacked him on the arm. "Holly's my best friend. Hands off. I get to take her out, not you."

"Ouch! I'm not doing anything wrong," Rupert said. "And she did save my life. We can all be friends together."

Alice stuck her tongue out at him. Her gaze shifted over his shoulder. "Oh, look! Your old café's hosting a 'make your own pot' event. We'll have to go to that. We'll make it a date. Just the two of us. No boys allowed." She shot a glare at Rupert and fluttered her lashes at Campbell.

I looked up at Rupert and shrugged. Our newly arranged date wasn't going to happen, after all. At least, not in the way he'd hoped. And maybe the way I hoped, too.

"That sounds like fun," I said. "Let's all go together, shall we? It's not nice leaving anyone out."

Alice's bottom lip jutted out. "Oh, very well. So long as Rupert doesn't walk around with a mopey face all the time."

"I don't have a mopey face," Rupert said.

"You do. You always look mopey when you don't get your own way. You're doing it now." She frowned and pulled her ears before puffing out her cheeks.

They started bickering, jabbing at each other, and pulling faces like children.

I stepped away and shook my head, my gaze lingering on my old café. It would be nice to drop in and have a discreet nose around. It was a change in the village, but it felt like a good change.

"Have you learned your lesson yet, Holmes?" Campbell's voice was so low that only I could hear him.

My spine straightened as I glanced at Alice and Rupert before turning to him. "What lesson do you think I need to learn?"

"That sticking your nose into things you're not an expert in leads to trouble."

"It also leads to solving crimes," I said, refusing to let my knees shake as he glared at me. "You should be thanking me."

"I have thanked you, by not having you arrested," he said. "I didn't charge you with interfering in an investigation, influencing witnesses, or tampering with evidence found at a crime scene."

I tutted. "I did none of that, and you know it. We were supposed to be partners in this investigation. Where were you when I was being stabbed? Aren't partners supposed to watch each other's backs?"

"I was doing my job. And if we really were partners, you should have informed me you were planning on confronting the suspects. Then I could have watched your back, front, and sides."

"I did try to find you, but you were busy. Rupert stepped in as my backup."

"Yes. We need to have a few words about what you think is appropriate backup in a dangerous situation," Campbell said. "Either that, or get you some training in how to defend yourself in a knife fight."

"Don't you dare suggest I start carrying around a gun," I said.

"I'd never dream of doing such a thing. You'd probably shoot yourself in the foot if you had one."

"More like I'd shoot you in the foot," I muttered.

"Holly, let's get a move on." Alice walked over and caught hold of my elbow. "I want to hear again about how you saved my brother and captured a killer."

I groaned and shook my head. "You've heard the story a dozen times. Aren't you bored yet?"

"How could I ever get bored with such an amazing story? Let's take a walk around the village green. And don't you dare leave out any details. Come along, Campbell. Keep up."

I glanced at him and grinned at his surly expression. Although there were some changes happening in Audley St. Mary, everything felt right again. I was surrounded by my friends, who I considered more like an extended family, I had my best dog by my side, and the sun was shining. Plus, Campbell hadn't yelled at me. It was a win-win all round.

Everything was right in the world. At least, everything felt right in our little corner of paradise. My home and my friends were safe once again.

About Author

K.E. O'Connor (Karen) is a cozy mystery author living in the beautiful British countryside. She loves all things mystery, animals, and cake (these often feature in her books.)

When she's not writing about mysteries, murder, and treats, she volunteers at a local animal sanctuary, reads a ton of books, binge watches mystery series on TV, and dreams about living somewhere warmer.

To stay in touch with the fun, clean mysteries, where the killer always gets their just desserts:

Newsletter: www.subscribepage.com/cozymysteries
Website: www.keoconnor.com/writing
Facebook: www.facebook.com/keoconnorauthor

Also By

Enjoy the complete Holly Holmes cozy culinary mysteries in paperback or e-book.

Cream Caramel and Murder

Chocolate Swirls and Murder

Vanilla Whip and Murder

Cherry Cream and Murder

Blueberry Blast and Murder

Mocha Cream and Murder

Lemon Drizzle and Murder

Maple Glaze and Murder

Mint Frosting and Murder

Read on for a peek at book five in the series - Blueberry Blast and Murder!

Chapter 1

I paused from loading the trolley on the back of my delivery bike as several wedding fair stallholders hurried past, their arms laden with stunning displays of flowers, the air alive with a heady floral scent.

"Woof, woof?" Meatball, my adorable corgi cross, bounced around my feet, wagging his tail.

"It's all go here again." I petted his head. "Is this wedding business making you think about finding the love of your life?"

He licked my hand, adoration in his large dark eyes.

I grinned and gave him a quick cuddle. "I feel the same. We don't need anyone else to be happy. You're my furry soulmate."

"Holly! Save me." Princess Alice Audley dashed across the courtyard, her long blonde hair flying out behind her and her cheeks flushed.

"What's the matter?" I looked over her shoulder. Was she being chased?

"It's my miserable cousin, Diana. Honestly, talk about a downer. She hasn't cracked a smile since she's been here. All she wants to do is talk about how awful men are now she's done with love. It's dismal."

I grinned and turned my attention to the trolley, securing the boxes of blueberry blast muffins on the back. "You can hardly blame her. She has just separated from her husband."

Alice gave a dramatic sigh. "You'd think it was the end of the world, not simply a failed marriage. Their relationship has been on the rocks for ages. Remember that enormous wedding anniversary celebration they had here? Even I could tell something was wrong between them." She sidled over to the bike. "What have you got in the boxes?"

"Nothing for you." I rested a hand on the top box. "I'm making a delivery to Artfully Homewares. Catherine is hosting a private party this afternoon and asked us to cater for it."

"I'm sure she won't mind if one cake is missing." Alice's hand crept toward the box.

I tapped the back of her hand. "You may be a princess, but you don't get to steal someone else's treats."

She huffed out a breath. "Very well. I'm much more excited about seeing your medieval decorated cake, anyway. How many layers has it got?"

I grinned at the mention of my baking. I'd been working on the cake for days, designing decorations and deciding on the final color scheme. "Five layers. It's looking good."

"It had better taste as good as it looks," Alice said. "And I want the first piece, since you're depriving me of these treats."

"The wedding fair will be open soon. There'll be loads of businesses giving away cake samples to lure people in. You can have your fill there."

"It won't be as delicious as yours. And I can't eat cake on my own in public. Imagine the headlines in the society pages: *'Princess Alice and Her Dismal Love Life.'* *'Princess Turns to Food for Comfort Because No One Will*

Marry Her.' And the pictures will show me stuffing myself with cake, all because I can't find a man."

"Maybe you'll get inspiration on how to find the perfect man at the wedding fair."

Alice turned and stared at the large marquees set up in the castle's grounds. "When I get married, I'm doing it barefoot on a beach, somewhere hot, where no one knows who I am. I'm not having all this fuss."

"I thought you wanted a huge wedding."

"I've changed my mind."

"Your parents won't approve. They'll want the wedding here." I gestured at Audley Castle. It was one of the prettiest castles in the country and had held a fair few grand weddings.

"So they can show me off like a prize peacock. All they care about is the connections my future husband will have." She scowled at the marquees. "What about love? Isn't that what marriage is supposed to be about?"

I adjusted the cake boxes. I was no expert when it came to love. I'd been single a long time. It usually didn't bother me, but seeing the wedding paraphernalia, it got me wondering. Maybe it was time I found a guy.

Meatball bounced off his front paws, his gaze on the trolley of treats.

"Meatball thinks you're being cruel by depriving us of those cakes," Alice said. "We can share one. I'm always happy to share with Meatball."

"You two can beg as much as you like. You're not getting these cakes. Here, have one of these." I passed her a leaflet.

"Plogging? Is this a spelling mistake?"

"No. It's something that started in Scandinavia. You combine jogging with cleaning up the countryside. It's popular over there. I'm planning an event after the wedding fair has finished. I thought we could get a few groups together and have a gentle jog around the beautiful countryside and make sure it's litter free. You're welcome to join in."

Her nose wrinkled. "I'm not a fan of running, or anything that makes me all sweaty and gross."

"It'll be gentle. You won't get a chance to go fast because you'll be stopping to pick up litter. You can get fit and clean up the environment."

"It doesn't sound too terrible," Alice said. "Okay, I'm in."

"You can be on my team. I'm hoping to recruit more people from the village. I figured I'd put up these leaflets and get some sign-ups. I'm already up to fifty. And I'll bake treats for people to eat at the end of the run. It'll be an incentive to get involved."

"Run! You said gentle jogging only." Alice's eyes narrowed. "You're not trying to trick me into some hideous extreme sport?"

I laughed. "Never. It'll be very gentle jogging. No sweating almost guaranteed."

"I could issue a decree so everyone in the village has to take part," Alice said.

"I'm hoping people will be happy to volunteer since it's for such a good cause," I said. "But if I'm low on numbers, I'll come back to you on the forced villager involvement."

"I'll be happy to twist arms. Well, get my security to do the rough stuff." She looked longingly at the boxes of cake. "Are you going to the catwalk event?"

"Nope. One wedding dress looks the same as all the others."

"No! You must come. I'm taking Diana, although I think it'll be a pointless exercise. I can't bear the thought of spending the evening with her while she cries over wedding dresses and her terrible marriage."

"So you want to burden me with that delight as well?"

Alice grinned at me. "That's what friends are for. We can share each other's pain. Plus, there'll be free champagne and canapés."

"I know! The kitchen is providing those canapés."

"Which means the food will be amazing. Come with me and Diana tomorrow evening. Between us, we can cheer her up. What else have you got planned?"

"Um, watching a cookery program?" I didn't exactly have a jam-packed social life.

"You can watch that any time. And if you get bored, you can always leave."

I sighed. Alice was hard to dissuade when she set her mind to something. "Sure. My exciting plans can wait."

"I'll get us front row seats," Alice said. "We can fill our faces with delicious food and laugh at all the flouncy gowns."

"It's a date. Now, I'd better get a move on. I need to get these cakes to Catherine." I scooped up Meatball, secured him in the basket on the front of the bike, and settled his safety helmet on his head.

"Bring me back a cake," Alice said. "I can smell how delicious they are."

"Go ask Chef Heston for a treat." I slung my leg over the bike. "I'll see you later." I pushed off and rounded the corner. I slammed on the brakes and a gasp shot out of me.

"Get your hands off me, you enormous oaf." A red-faced, red-haired woman was being held securely by Campbell Milligan, the castle's head of security.

"You've been warned before. I told you not to come back." Campbell strode along, tugging the woman beside him.

"You don't own this place. I can come here if I like. I paid the visitor entry fee. I haven't even had a chance to look around the wedding fair."

"You're not welcome."

"What's going on?" I asked as I wheeled my bike toward them.

"It's nothing to do with you." Campbell glanced at me, his stern features hardening.

"Get him off me," the woman said. "I'm innocent. He's being a bully."

I knew Campbell well enough to know he'd never bully anyone. I cycled along beside them. "Campbell can be protective of the family. Did you do something to upset them?"

"I'm not interested in the Audley family or this tedious drafty castle," the woman said.

"Then why is he making you leave?" I asked.

"Holly, go about your business. It looks like you have a delivery to make." Campbell glared at me.

"I do. But we're heading in the same direction. I can keep you company." And find out why he was dragging this angry woman to the exit.

"Not anymore we aren't." He abruptly turned and headed toward a different exit.

I put my foot on the ground as he strode away, the woman still complaining as he tugged her along. I was impressed by the fight she was putting up. Campbell was twice her size and not to be messed with.

I was just pushing off again to head into the village, when I spotted a tall, elegant woman wearing large dark glasses, a green scarf over her hair. I could have been mistaken, but it looked like she'd been watching the argument between Campbell and the woman. Although now, she seemed focused on me.

I slowly raised a hand. There was something familiar about her. Did I know her? It was hard to see her features from this distance.

The second she saw me lift my hand, she turned and disappeared around the side of the castle.

If she was up to no good, Campbell would soon be chasing her down as well. There were so many people here as part of the wedding fair that it wasn't unusual to find them lost and confused, stumbling into places they shouldn't.

"Let's get a move on, Meatball. It'll be good to get away from this chaos for an hour."

"Woof, woof!" His bark was full of agreement as we headed out of the castle gates and along the empty lanes toward Audley St. Mary, my pretty village home.

Although I often complained about the hills that led into the village, I always got a good workout when I used the bike to make deliveries. The burn in my thighs told me my muscles were definitely working hard today.

Meatball loved being in the bike basket. He was secured inside so he couldn't jump out, but he could sit back, place his front paws over the front of the basket and get an excellent view as I cycled along.

I waved at several villagers as I headed toward the stores. Audley St. Mary had a great range of small independent stores that had a thriving trade. There were a few chain stores and restaurants, one of which was a café I never entered, considering it put my own café out of business not so long ago.

And that was where I was headed. My former café was home to Artfully Homewares, and I was happy to see it thriving.

I stopped the bike and climbed off. I unbuckled my helmet and flipped it over the handles of the bike, scooped Meatball out, and removed his helmet, before placing him on the ground.

"Holly! What are you doing away from the castle?"

I turned at the sound of Lord Rupert Audley's voice and smiled at him. "I've got a delivery to make. What about you?"

He sighed and stuffed his hands into his pockets. "I'm hiding."

"From what?"

"Ever since the wedding fair started, I've had several long, intensely awkward conversations with my mother. She keeps talking about my wedding."

I gritted my teeth and winced. "Your wedding! Is there someone you're interested in marrying?"

"Several eligible bachelorettes have been mentioned," Rupert said glumly.

My stomach flip-flopped. I'd had a bit of a crush on Rupert for a long time. "Have any of these bachelorettes taken your eye?"

"They're all lovely girls, but not what I'm interested in." He glanced at me and pushed his messy blond hair off his face. "I mean, I know I need to settle down. Grow up, as my mother keeps telling me, but why can't things stay the same? We're happy as we are, aren't we?"

"I mean, sure. You seem happy enough. Although maybe you could meet someone who'll make you happier."

He grinned. "You make me happy. Especially when you come laden with delicious looking treats in boxes."

I chuckled and shook my head. "No chance. Your sister tried to pull the same stunt when she saw these cakes. This is a delivery for Catherine in the pottery store."

"Oh! Well, why don't we both go in? We can have a browse while we're here."

"I can't be long. I need to get back to the castle. I'm making the finishing touches to my medieval cake design."

"Alice was telling me all about that. It sounds exciting. Can't you spare half an hour away from the kitchen? You deserve a break. I bet Chef Heston's been working you too hard as usual."

"He always does." Being around Rupert put a smile on my face. He was always thinking about other people and making sure they were happy. "You're right. Half an hour won't hurt."

"I'll give you a hand in with the boxes." Rupert unclipped the boxes and lifted up two.

I grabbed the rest, and we headed into the store, Meatball trotting beside me.

Catherine Miquel looked up from her position behind the reclaimed oak counter, the counter I had fitted when this was my café. She had warm brown eyes, a friendly smile, and often had a paintbrush tucked behind one ear. "Holly! And ... goodness. Lord Rupert. This is an unexpected surprise. Do you normally make deliveries for the castle, your ... lordship?"

He chuckled. "This is a special occasion. And call me Rupert. I'm just helping Holly out."

Catherine's eyes widened as she looked at me. "That's nice of you. Come through the back, you can put the cakes in the kitchen."

I grinned. "I know the way. Is it okay to have Meatball in here? He's well-behaved. He probably thinks of this place as a second home."

"Of course. He's welcome." Catherine strode ahead of us, holding open the doors so we could get through with the boxes.

Although the place had a familiar feel, it looked so different. Catherine had painted the walls a bright yellow and added extra shelving in the front for the pots people could make in the store. There was also a large display cabinet at the back and the counter had been moved.

When I entered the kitchen, I was surprised to see a large kiln in one corner.

I set the boxes down, my gaze roving over the room. It was different, but I approved. A lot of care and love had gone into making this place beautiful.

"Thanks for bringing these over," Catherine said. "One of the ladies in the village is having a birthday party here this afternoon. She said she wanted some extra special treats. Of course, I instantly thought of the castle kitchen and all the delicious desserts you make."

"I'm glad you did," Rupert said. "Holly's the best baker we've ever had. We plan to make sure she stays with us forever."

I glanced at him and grinned. "You're very kind. Everyone else in the kitchen is also capable of making nice cakes."

"Oh, absolutely! You just do those special finishing touches that make your cakes magic," Rupert said.

"I'm thrilled to have the cakes for the party," Catherine said. "Have you got time to stop for a cup of tea?"

"We hoped you'd say that." Rupert rubbed his hands together. "And I wouldn't mind having a go at painting a pot while I'm here."

Catherine's hand fluttered against her chest. "Of course. It would be my honor to host you."

"Only if it's no bother," I said. "You do have the party to sort out."

"It's no trouble. The party doesn't start for another few hours. I'm almost set up and ready to go. You're welcome to try your hand at pottery painting. Would you like to try, too, Holly?"

"I would. Thanks."

"We came for a look around not long after you opened," Rupert said. "I brought my sister and Holly. Alice was showing off her painting skills, so I didn't get a look in when it came to having a go."

"I remember." Catherine brewed up tea and set out some mugs. "Your sister's visit to the store drew quite an audience."

"She always does that," Rupert said. "She's a right show off."

"I was grateful for the publicity." Catherine poured the tea. "We were on the front page of the newspapers for several weeks, and I've been booked solid ever since. An endorsement from the Audley family is always good for business."

"Well, I suppose Alice has her uses." Rupert accepted a mug of tea.

I nodded a thanks at Catherine as she passed me a mug. "It looks like the store's doing really well."

"It is. I'm thrilled," Catherine said. "I always dreamed of owning my own pottery and homeware store. I couldn't miss the opportunity when I discovered this place. And the villagers have been so welcoming."

"It's why I love it here," I said.

"Let me take you through to the store." Catherine walked to the kitchen door. "You can have a look at the pots available for painting. I'll bring out a few of these cakes for you to enjoy as well."

Rupert grinned like an overexcited child. "That sounds perfect. Come on, Holly." He took hold of my arm and guided me into the store.

I didn't miss the surprised look on Catherine's face as he escorted me out.

My relationship with the Audley family was unique. I considered myself privileged to be included in their friendship group but understood how odd it seemed to others. A kitchen assistant being friends with a lord and a princess. Sometimes, I couldn't get my head around it, either. But it just worked.

We were soon settled at the table, paint brushes in hand, cakes beside us, and two small pots awaiting their final design. Meatball was settled by my feet.

"This is the life," Rupert said. "This is all I need to be happy. A strong mug of tea, a delicious cake, and you."

My eyebrows shot up. "Me?"

He glanced up, his cheeks flaming. "I mean, a good friend. You understand? I mean, you're not just a friend. You're ... well, you're special. You make Audley Castle special."

I looked away, my gaze going to Meatball, who sat patiently by the table, no doubt hoping for some cake. "How about we paint these pots?"

"Yes. Right. Let's get to work." He grinned and ducked his head.

If only I could date Rupert. Although if I did, life would get a lot more complicated, and I was happy with my current situation.

Cake, tea, and my best furry buddy by my side. It wasn't a bad way to live.

Blueberry Blast and Murder is available to buy in paperback or e-book format.

ISBN: 978-1-9163573-4-1

Here are two more treats. Enjoy these delicious cherry-themed recipes (brownies and cobbler.) Chef Heston approved!

Recipe – Cherry and Chocolate Brownies

Prep time: 15 minutes **Cook time:** 35 minutes

Stays fresh for 3 days, or in the freezer for 3 months.

Recipe can be made dairy and egg-free. Substitute milk for a plant/nut alternative, use dairy-free spread, and mix 3 tbsp flaxseed with 1 tbsp water to create one flax 'egg' as a binding agent (this recipe requires 9 tbsp flaxseed to substitute the 3 eggs.)

INGREDIENTS
1/2 cup (140g) unsalted butter room temperature
1.5 cups (300g) sugar
3 large eggs
1 cup (125g) plain flour
3/4 cup (75g) cocoa powder
½ tsp salt
½ tsp baking powder
3/4 cup (75g) dark chocolate
1.8 cups (250g) pitted cherries cut into quarters

INSTRUCTIONS

1. Preheat oven to 340F (170C). Butter the bottom and sides of your 8-inch square tin or line with baking paper.

2. In a saucepan, combine the butter and 1 cup (100g) of sugar and heat, stirring until the sugar has dissolved and the butter melted. Set aside.

3. In a large bowl, whisk the eggs and remaining sugar until light, smooth, and fluffy. Pour the sugar and butter mixture into the sugar and egg mixture and whisk.

4. In a medium bowl mix flour, cocoa powder, baking powder, and salt. Add to the sugar, egg, and butter mix and whisk. Do not overmix.

5. Add the chocolate and cherries and fold in.

6. Pour the batter into the prepared baking tin.

7. Bake for 35 minutes or until the top of the brownies is set, with few cracks.

8. Remove from oven.

9. Allow the brownies to completely cool before eating – if you can!

Bonus Recipe – Cherry Cobbler

Prep time: 20 minutes **Cook time:** 45 minutes

Keeps for 3-4 days.

Recipe can be dairy and egg-free. Substitute milk for a plant alternative, use dairy-free spread, and mix 3 tbsp flaxseed with 1 tbsp water to create a flax 'egg' as a binder (this recipe needs 3 tbsp flaxseed to substitute 1 egg.)

INGREDIENTS
6 cups (approx. 600g - to fill the dish) cherries
2/3 cup (135g) sugar
1 tbsp lemon juice
1/4 cup (35g) all-purpose flour
Topping:
2 1/2 (350g) cup all-purpose flour
1 tsp baking powder
2 1/2 tablespoons sugar, plus more for sprinkling
1 1/2 sticks (170g) + 2 tbsp of salted butter, cut into pieces
3/4 cup (240g) milk
1 large egg

INSTRUCTIONS

1. Preheat the oven to 425F (210C)

2. Put cherries in a bowl and sprinkle with sugar and lemon juice.

3. Add the flour and stir to combine.

4. In a separate bowl, combine flour, baking powder, sugar, and salt. Stir.

5. Add 1 1/2 sticks of cold butter and use a blender to cut the butter into the dry ingredients (or a knife and cold fingers.)

6. Whisk the milk and egg, then add to the mixture and stir until the dough comes together. It should be clumpy.

7. Pour the cherries into a 9 x 13-inch baking dish and add 2 tbsp butter.

8. Take lumps of the dough and place them over the cherries.

9. Sprinkle the top with sugar.

10. Cover with foil and bake for 20 minutes, then remove the foil and bake for 20 minutes.

11. Serve warm with ice cream (try not to eat it all in one go, but I won't tell if you do!)

Made in the USA
Las Vegas, NV
21 October 2022

57817361R00143